Temporary Bride

Arabella Sheen

Can Amy let go of the past and face an unknown future with Max?

Max Jordan is one of America's most powerful, leading corporate lawyers. He is also the major stockholder and head of the billion-dollar corporation - Jordan Diamond Empire.
Max must marry soon to keep the business safe and the company secure from a takeover.

Returning to England in search of the only woman he knows and trusts to help him in his moment of need - he tracks Amy down and asks her to marry him.

Amy Denver wants nothing to do with Max Jordan…and she certainly wants nothing to do with his marriage proposal. Five painful years have passed since Max disappeared from her life and a lot has happened to her in between. Amy has a secret she'd rather he didn't discover…her secret is Jake…their son. Once again Amy finds herself surrendering to Max and his demands as he whisks her and Jake off to Waterfront, his private, secluded home in the Hamptons.

Chapter 1

Dawn was breaking on the horizon of the London skyline as Max Jordan, head and company director of Jordan Diamond Empire, flew into Heathrow airport in his private jet.

It had been a long, arduous North Atlantic flight but Max had spent his hours in the air lucratively. During the flight, he'd been fighting a mid-air battle using his laptop and he'd won a diamond laser contract for his company worth billions of dollars. All that remained to be done was for him to fly to Japan and finalise the deal with a face-to-face handshake and a signature on the dotted line.

Looking at Max, no one would guess he hadn't slept in nearly twenty-four hours. Having had a quick shower on the plane and changed into one of his many handmade suits, he looked as fleshly groomed and as sleek as he had hours earlier when he'd boarded the luxury jet in New York.

Tall, tanned and dynamic, Max could be described as sex on legs.

Ploughing his way through the VIP lounge to the waiting limousine outside, all eyes turned in his direction. Chic, stylishly-beautiful women followed him with desire in their eyes, while waiting businessmen revealed a flash of envy as he passed. But Max was oblivious to all their stares. He was a man on a mission and time was of the essence.

The door to the limousine was being held open in readiness for him and, without ceremony, Max sped passed the onlookers and climbed into the back seat. Pulling away from the airport the chauffeur looked in the driving mirror and asked, "Where to Mr. Jordan? Your hotel or the office?"

"Office please," Max replied. He then proceeded to indulge in a luxury he never normally found time for…he sat back and let himself experience the ride.

The laptop and briefcase he'd brought along with him lay unnoticed and forgotten on the seat beside him and, as he sat back looking out of the window watching familiar landmarks go by, he felt a pang of nostalgia for the old times.

After five years of absence from the city, he was once more back in London and vivid memories of happier times came flooding back. It had been a carefree period in his life when he could do exactly as he wished. Now things were different. He had responsibilities.

Max still called the shots and had ultimate power and control of the business, but in some things, his hands were bound and tied.

Often he felt the weight of his obligations heavy on his shoulders, and that was one of the reasons he was here today in London.

He was here to perform a duty…*his duty*.

He needed a wife and he knew what he had to do.

Max had returned to England to find and marry Amy Denver.

* * * *

Without any problems, the limo cut through the city's heavy morning traffic and when it reached a tall building where Martin and Campbell had their law offices, Max stepped out of the car and was immediately greeted by an entourage of eager people. A welcoming party had been patiently waiting on tenterhooks for his arrival.

A zealous individual willing to please Max gathered the laptop and briefcase from the car and Max was politely steered towards a rank of open lifts which were all being held in anticipation of his arrival.

"We've been expecting you, sir. How was your flight?"

"The flight was good thank you…long, but good. Now, perhaps one of you would like to show me around your firm before the meeting. I'd like to get a feel for the place and see how you run your operation." He was taking control of the situation.

Max glanced pointedly at the sleek, slim watch on his wrist and everyone took the hint.

They all stepped into the waiting lifts and, with the doors closed securely behind them, they went straight to the fifth floor where Martin and Campbell had their offices.

Max was in London on two accounts - company and personal business.

He was working with the English law firm Martin and Campbell on an international lawsuit involving worldwide diamond embezzling. But the diamond lawsuit wasn't his only reason for being in London…he was here for more. He wanted to find Amy Denver and take her back to America with him, only Amy didn't know that…yet.

Jordan Diamond Empire was in trouble and if Max didn't marry soon to protect the company, he might not have a company to run.

On the sixth floor, Amy was blissfully unaware of Max Jordan's presence in the building. In the conference room, she was busy laying out files and briefs on the long, wooden, mahogany table and generally preparing for the onslaught of lawyers who were about to descend on her.

Catching a glimpse of herself in the reflective shine of the conference room window, Amy smoothed her hair back into place and straightened her pencil-slim, black skirt over the smooth, slender, sexy curves of her hips.

She was ready to face the barrage of lawyers heading her way.

She knew she looked good and she felt good. Adrenaline was pumping in her veins and she was ready to take on the world.

In the four years, Amy had been with the law firm as a junior lawyer she'd been faultlessly brilliant in her work. She excelled at her job and there was no one with better skills to run and manage the support teams.

It was her ability to organise and cope in any difficult situation that had won the hearts of her colleagues and she was greatly valued by them all.

"Is everything under control Amy?" Peering around the door was Cathy Moore.

Cathy was one of the female partners who had also become a good friend of Amy's.

"Sure…everything's fine. Why what's up?" Amy asked.

"The American's here. The whole place is buzzing with the news and it seems they're now heading here to the conference room." There was an urgency in Cathy's voice.

Cathy was showing concern for the controlled chaos that seemed to be rampant throughout the building.

"Well that's good news," said Amy brightly. "Hopefully we'll be sticking to our schedule and we'll have no delays. For once maybe…just maybe, I'll be able to get away from work on time."

"You'll be lucky," said Cathy letting out a deep sigh. "We'll probably all have to stay and work overtime. I imagine we'll be here slogging away until midnight catching up on any decisions they make during the meeting."

Amy let out a long agonising groan.

"Don't worry. I'm sure James will let you leave early. But right now I've got to go…see you later." With a quick wave, Cathy disappeared from sight.

Amy hadn't thought about the extra hours she might have to work this evening and she felt uneasy about having to stay on longer than planned.

The full-on meeting was due to take place in ten minutes and anyone of importance had to attend.

Today of all day's there was no room for error. It was decision day and the partners were going to determine which of them would be working with Max Jordan and take on the Diablo case.

Rumour had it James Martin - the senior partner - was likely to take the job. It was James who had brought the American lawyer in on the case and this new guy was supposed to be an expert in the field of diamonds and corporate law.

From somewhere along the corridor Amy heard a scurry of foot-falls approaching. It was her boss James Martin and his team.

"Good morning Amy," James said giving her a conspiratorial wink.

She saw he was wearing his blue shirt and tie which meant James was in a good mood and ready for action.

"James, morning…nice to see you," she said enthusiastically and greeted him with her usual sunny smile.

Four years ago James had sat in on her interview. Throughout the years he had mentored her and encouraged her to work hard. Little by little she'd climbed and worked her way up the corporate ladder. She thought of James as the older brother she never had. But James liking what he saw, was continually trying his luck and asked Amy out on numerous occasions. Every time she refused, he took it on the chin and waited…until the next time.

"We're ready when you are sir," she said politely.

Everything was in place and ready for the meeting. The white marker board had been cleaned and the new digital hologram projection system was set-up and running.

Nearly everyone had arrived and were ready to take their seats and prepare for the onslaught of questions. They were, however, still waiting for the infamous American lawyer to appear.

Everyone was on tenterhooks expecting his arrival at any minute and even James, who was rarely flustered, seemed on edge.

At that moment, the door to the conference room opened and a tall, forceful figure appeared framed in the doorway.

Amy felt the blood drain from her face.

Gripping the back of a nearby chair for support, she just managed to stop herself from fainting.

Max Jordan - *her Max Jordan* - was standing in the doorway and Max looked like he owned the place.

Amy hadn't realised Jordan Diamond Empire and Max were linked. It was a shock to her system and she was only just starting to put two and two together.

The jacket of Max's dark business suit was open revealing the crisp white of his silk shirt and tie, and his hands were thrust deep into his trouser pockets. Tall, muscular and with wide, broad shoulders he practically filled the doorway.

Amy at five-seven in stockinged feet was considered to be quite tall, but she was nothing compared to the six-foot-two giant who was deliberately and unhurriedly advancing towards her.

She was standing near James and Max came to a stop when he reached the person he'd travelled all this way to see. He'd found what he wanted…he'd found Amy.

Slowly she dared to look up at him. In his eyes, she saw a glint of victory and something else…something that looked like an achievement…a triumph.

Amy's felt fearful.

She was looking at a man she thought she would never see again and it was as if the years in between slipped away. As she looked at him, she was once more a young trainee law student at university and Max was a handsome newly-qualified lawyer from America.

She'd been innocent, naïve and emotionally vulnerable and she'd fallen totally and completely head-over-heels in love with him. She'd been such a fool and she'd no idea how she could have been so mistaken all those years ago.

Max looked at her knowingly. He too was remembering those days.

He was the same man, but different. He'd aged. They both had.

Looking closely at Max she could see he was beginning to grey slightly at the temples. Before, when she'd known him, his hair had been jet black. Now lines were etched on his face, but they were character lines that simply added to his charisma and charm.

Max Jordan was still a compelling and magnetic man and she could still feel the allure of his sexual magnetism. Stood before her was not the young lawyer she'd once known. Here was a dynamic man of the world.

Once he'd been her world. Her life had revolved around him…and now…now she wanted absolutely nothing to do with Max.

James Martin's voice broke the silence in the room.

"Max let me welcome you to our turf. It's good to have you here. Everybody…allow me to introduce Max Jordan of Jordan Diamond. Max is here today to lend us his legal expertise in the Diablo case," he said.

Going around the group James introduced Max to the team. Then it was Amy's turn to be formally introduced.

James was ignorant of the fact that Amy had known Max before today. She'd kept him in the dark about the relationship and she was now wondering if that had been a wise decision.

"Amy's been with us quite some time. How long has it been Amy…three…four years?" James asked.

Amy didn't answer. She couldn't answer.

James had been talking about her, paying her compliments and telling Max how good she was at her job and all the time she hadn't heard a word James had said. She'd been staring at Max in total surprise and horror.

She was amazed he was here in this very room. She could even reach out and touch him if she wanted to…but she didn't.

"Hello, Amy?" His deep drawl was still the same, just as she remembered. She hadn't forgotten. She could never forget that sexy American accent.

Then before she realised what he intended to do, Max stepped forward and reached out to clasp her hand. Pulling her gently, but forcefully towards him, he planted a soft lingering kiss on her surprised, open lips.

"You two know each other?" James asked. He was somewhat taken aback.

"Amy and I go way back," Max explained and he raised an eyebrow suggestively.

Amy felt a blush of embarrassment covering her face and it was there for all to see.

Max was still holding her hand and she knew he could feel her body trembling. She was shaking from head to toe, dreading what was about to come.

Max Jordan wasn't supposed to be here.

He was supposed to be out of her life. He was supposed to be somewhere on the other side of the world…not here in England.

Feeling fenced in, she began to panic. She had to get away from him. She felt she couldn't stay there a moment longer.

Amy was about to make a run for it but Max gripped and held her tightly against his side. Now that he'd found her, it seemed he wasn't letting go.

"What? You two know each other? Amy, you dark horse," James said. "You could have warned us you knew Max."

"Oh no, I don't know Max. I mean…I don't know Mr. Jordan," Amy spluttered, trying to keep her composure.

She was frantically denying the fact she knew Max. Looking around the room she tried to convince everyone she was telling the truth.

"We were only briefly acquainted," she explained. "And I never really knew him."

And then she said something unforgivable. "And I don't need and I don't want to know him now."

She heard a sharp intake of air as Max drew in his breath through clenched teeth.

It seemed she'd hit a nerve.

She'd gone too far and, although she was dismayed at what she'd unthinkingly said, she couldn't and wouldn't take the words back.

They were true.

She'd never really known the true Max and she didn't want to get to know him again. She'd too much to lose. She was aiming to avoid Max at all costs.

"You always did have a reputation of saying what you thought," Max said smiling.

"Oh, so now I have a reputation. And what sort of reputation would that be Mr. Jordan? A ruined reputation?"

The sarcasm was dripping from her tongue and Max made a face as if she'd just wounded him deeply.

What right did he have to look at her like that? She was the injured party. Not him.

She desperately wanted to leave and get away but she couldn't. With the room full of lawyers waiting for her to start the meeting, there was no chance of an immediate escape.

She was forced to stay.

Max was still holding her against his side and discreetly she started tugging away from him until reluctantly he had to release her. As their contact was broken she felt his energy draining from her.

"Ladies and gentlemen please be seated." Max was taking command of the meeting. "I believe we're to have a presentation followed by a discussion," he said. "If everyone's here…shall we proceed?"

On shaky legs and with some difficulty, Amy went over to the hologram projector and started operating the high-tech equipment.

She gave the opening speech flawlessly and when her presentation of the facts had ended the senior partners took over. Then they started getting down to the nitty-gritty.

When discussions finished it was unanimously decided Max was the best man to represent both sides of the Atlantic. He was the lawyer who was going to present the case to the English and American judicial systems. He was the man for the job.

With everyone anticipating a long, complicated, legal battle that could take months of court appearances and high powered negotiations, concerns were voiced about the amount of travelling Max would have to do. But Max shrugged off their worries telling them travel wasn't a problem for him.

As Max began closing the meeting he stood up to address the group.

"Well, that seems to be it," he told them. "I believe we've covered the most urgent points on the agenda and I'd like to say thanks for giving me such a warm welcome to Martin and Campbell earlier. I think I now have some insight into how things work here and where to go if I'm in trouble. And as I'm always in trouble, you'll probably be seeing a lot of me."

There was a burst of shared laughter from his audience.

"Officially I'm not one of the team but at some point, I shall probably need one of you to help me with my legal work when I'm in England. I'd like someone who knows the ropes and can *organise me*. Someone who can do the legwork so to speak."

At the back of the room, someone mumbled something and a chuckle of agreement came from various staff members.

"Amy has great legs."

Max had heard what was said and Amy saw his lips curve into a grin of agreement.

Didn't the man miss anything?

Max was waiting expectantly for someone to volunteer and then he said, "Someone has just kindly suggested Amy and, if there are no objections, I'd like Amy to work with me whilst I'm here."

"Who wouldn't want Amy?" It was the same voice and everyone laugh again.

Everyone, that is, except Amy.

The whole room was waiting to gauge James's reaction to Max's request. James simply shrugged his shoulders offering no objections.

"If it's alright with Amy, it's alright with me," he replied.

Amy panicked.

"I'm sure I can find someone from the typing pool to assist Mr. Jordan," she offered hurriedly. "And if there are any problems he can…"

"No, it's alright. Max can have you," said James Martin laying down the law.

Amy knew there would be no arguing with James. A decision had been made.

"Max will have a heavy workload and he'll need all the help he can get. You're the best we've got Amy." James had turned to look at her.

Max can have you.

She didn't like the sound of that. How dare they pass her about as if she was a slave to be bartered with?

She was totally opposed to working with Max but that didn't seem to matter to anyone. It seemed Max was being handed what he wanted on a plate…and he wanted Amy.

Unwillingly and reluctantly Amy had to agree that logically the decision was the right one.

If they hoped to achieve the impossible and win the Diablo case, Max would need all the help he could get and she was the most suitable assistant for the job.

When the meeting was over and everyone was leaving, Amy made a quick dash and escaped to her own office.

She was on the point of collapse and could scarcely stand.

All she wanted to do was close her office door and shut out the world. However, when she turned around to do just that, she found Max had followed her from the conference room and was now standing behind. He towered over her and she almost buckled at the knees.

Now he had her cornered in her office. For the first time in five years, she was once again alone with Max Jordan.

"Not now Max, please," she said, almost begging.

"Amy, at some point we have to talk," he told her bluntly. "I'll leave you to choose the time and the place if you like. If you want somewhere that's private, that's fine. But we need to talk. We have unfinished business."

He wasn't asking her. He was telling her. And there was no question he would get what he wanted.

Max had walked back into her life and he wasn't being quite about it.

"We've nothing to talk about Max. Either privately or in public," she said sternly.

She was determined to avoid being alone with him at all costs.

"I'll work with you during office hours," she told him. "But only because I have to. If you want to talk to me about anything other than what we're working on, I'm not interested. I'm not going to listen to you and I don't want to know."

Max simple ignored what she'd just said.

"I have a full day ahead of me with James and I'm not sure when we'll be finished." He looked quickly at his watch. "We ought to get through the case notes by about five o'clock. I'll look in here after we've finished and we can…"

"I won't be here," she told him in no uncertain terms. "And I'm not waiting."

"You never did wait. Did you? That was one of our problems." He shook his head in frustration and took a deep breath. "If you're not here how do I get hold of you?"

"You don't…I'll call you."

She smiled a tight smile as if her face would crack.

He got the message. He knew she wouldn't be calling him. She didn't have his mobile number and he realised she wouldn't make an effort to get in contact.

"Although you might think it, I wasn't born yesterday. Give me your number and I'll phone you," he demanded.

She wasn't giving him her number at any costs. She didn't want anything to do with him and there was absolutely no way she going to become involved with him for a second time.

As far as she was concerned the past was over and done with. She'd moved on and she'd started a new life.

"Amy! What's your number?" he barked out threateningly between clenched teeth. "Tell me…"

She was brought back to reality with a jerk.

Quickly she found a scrap of paper and scribbled her number on it before unwillingly handing it over. She felt like she'd just signed her life away.

"I'll be here at five. Wait for me," and then he was gone.

With her head in a spin from the whirlwind of events that morning, Amy pressed a button on her desk putting the switchboard on hold and left her office.

Passing reception she entered the nearby stationary store cupboard where the surplus office equipment was kept and, slamming the door shut behind her, she burst into tears sobbing inconsolably.

Everyone, even the most junior members of staff, knew you never went into the stationary store cupboard if the door was shut.

It wasn't until fifteen minutes later, when Cathy came to grab a quick cup of coffee and a gossip with Amy about the meeting, that it was discovered she was still nowhere to be seen. She hadn't returned to her office.

Cathy went in search of her friend and was pointed in the direction of the store cupboard by one of the reception staff.

Tapping on the door and receiving no reply Cathy cautiously turned the handle and found Amy with a very damp handkerchief mopping her eyes and vigorously blowing her red nose.

Amy looked up and saw her friend.

"Oh Cathy…" she cried, before once again collapsing into a snivelling wreck. "I never cry…never…not even when Jake had meningitis and we couldn't bring his temperature down. And the time I sprained my ankle and I couldn't walk for a week. I never cry."

"I know…I know," said Cathy soothingly. "But sometimes we need to cry."

"But you don't know. You can't know what's happened," Amy sniffed loudly.

"No, I don't. But whatever it is, it will be alright. Nothing can be that bad. Except if something's happened to Jake. Nothing's happened to him…has it?" Cathy asked.

All of a sudden Amy turned as white as the stack of A4 sheets of paper piled in front of her on the storeroom shelves.

"Jake? No, it's not Jake At least…he's supposed to be in day school. No, it Jake's father. He's found us. Max is here," she cried.

"Max? Max Jordan?" Cathy said reeling from the shock.

"Cathy, you've set alarm bells ringing. I've got to call the school and see if Jake's alright. I have to see if he's still there. He might have been taken. I wouldn't put it past Max to…"

But Cathy didn't hear the remainder of what Amy was saying. Amy had already left the store cupboard and was running to her office where she frantically dialled the number of Jake's school. Her hands were shaking.

The school reassured her Jake was still in class and he wouldn't be leaving until she came to collect him.

Putting down the phone Amy sank into her office chair and put her head in her hands.

"Drink," Cathy said as she put a steaming cup of tea on the desk in front of Amy.

Amy picked up the cup and did as she was told. She took a few sips of the hot, sweet, steamy liquid and made a face.

"You know I don't take sugar," Amy said grimacing.

"It will do you good and whilst you are drinking it you can tell me what's going on," Cathy said firmly.

Then the two friends sat and talked together for a while.

"So you see Max came, he saw, and he conquered…and then he deserted. Well not literally. It's just that other things probably got in his way," Amy explained. She'd no idea why she was making excuses for the man.

When Cathy heard the story Amy had just told, she didn't see, or couldn't see and wouldn't see, how anyone would willingly leave beautiful, gentle Amy.

Only a fool would have walked away when Amy had given him her heart.

* * * *

It all happened five years ago when Amy had been training as a law student at the university. Her parents had died in a head-on collision with another car and, although the accident had been no one's fault, Amy had been left devastated by their deaths.

Fellow students had become her family. They had supported and pulled her through the rough times. And then Max had come into her life.

They met one afternoon in the law office where she'd been working as a work placement student. Max was a practising lawyer in America at the time, but he'd come to England to gain experience in International Commercial Law before returning to his practice in New York.

The ever-so organised Max had his career mapped out before him. Working in England in a specialist field was an opportunity that was supposed to be going to make or break his career.

Nothing and no one was going to stop him on his pathway to success. He was focussed and career-minded, and then along came Amy.

Amy had never been quite sure about Max's family life or what he did when he was in America, but his family history hadn't mattered and she'd never really pushed for details.

But perhaps she should have.

She'd been in love with him. Totally. And who he was or where he came from seemed unimportant to her then.

Max used to say his nomadic career style and moving from country to country was an invaluable life experience. What she hadn't realised was that she too was part of that nomadic learning curve.

It seemed their relationship had been temporary and Max, for whatever reason, had eventually chosen to move on with his life.

They'd had one brief, glorious, hot summer together and then she'd had nothing. He'd utterly seduced her and she'd been willingly his for the taking. And Max had taken all that she'd offered, leaving her with only the memories.

For six red-hot, steamy, passionate months they had lived together in her compact, one-bedroom apartment not far from the university.

Together they would come home from a long, hard day's work at the office and it would be an even longer, harder night in bed until the early hours of the morning,

At night they would fall asleep, sweaty and exhausted in each other's arms until she was woken in the dawn's early light by his urgent need of her. They couldn't get enough of one another and their bodies craved fulfilment from one another, like a drug.

He'd used her but not unkindly. And when she looked back on their time together she realised she'd only herself to blame.

She'd been full of innocence and she'd been trusting. Her naivety hadn't been his fault...only hers.

When Max's time in England was at an end he'd asked her to go back with him to America, but she couldn't. The time wasn't right. She had a law degree to finish.

Amy had been studying for nearly five years and they both thought it would be stupid to throw it all away for the sake of a few months.

He'd said she could always join him later - after her exams were over - but it hadn't worked out that way.

She'd been so sure of his love that as soon as she'd finished her exams, she caught the first available flight to America and had flown there with the intention of living with him.

It was to have been a surprise, but the only person who had been surprised was Amy.

Flying into New York International Airport at two in the morning she'd been jet-lagged, tired and wanting nothing more than the open arms of Max. Only she couldn't fall into his waiting arm. He wasn't there and no one seemed to know where he was.

The night watchman in the apartment complex where he was staying let her in, but only as far as the lobby. She'd never been in such a place before. There was marble from floor to ceiling and everything that was chrome or crystal gleamed.

"I'm here to see Max Jordan," she explained to the night watchman.

"Mr. Jordan? Is he expecting you, Miss?" he asked politely.

"No, he isn't. I'm afraid I've only just landed," Amy explained.

The security guard looked questioningly at the flight bag she was carrying and the off-the-peg jeans she was wearing. Her luggage and clothing weren't designer labelled and it was obvious to her that anyone entering these portals would usually have 'chic' written all over them. She didn't. She was wearing her comfortable travelling gear.

"If you could buzz him, I'm sure he wouldn't mind seeing me," she said bravely and pointed to the elaborate intercom system.

"Buzz him? I'm sorry, Miss. There would be no point in buzzing Mr. Jordan. The gentleman's not here," he explained apologetically.

"Could you say when he's likely to be home?" she asked.

"Don't know. It could be tomorrow…could be in a couple of months. Last week he packed a bag and the limo took him to the airport. He didn't say when he'd be back, Miss. If you'd like to leave a note I can see that it gets left with his mail. But I can't say when or even if he'll get it, Miss. The Jordans have closed the New York apartment until further notice."

Amy was feeling totally alienated and out of her depth. To make it worse, when she made enquiries at the place where Max was supposed to be working, she was told there had been a family emergency and that he couldn't be contacted.

That was probably the reason he hadn't been answering his mobile phone.

She was faced with the fact Max wasn't here and no one was prepared to say when, or even if, he was coming back to New York.

Without a green card, she couldn't get work and although she'd sat her law exams, the exam results weren't out and she'd no proof of her qualifications.

Any money she had with her would soon run out and she couldn't rely on Max returning in the near future.

With no qualifications, no work and nowhere to stay, she had no other option than to return to England.

Reluctantly she caught the next flight home intending to wait for Max to contact her.

He didn't.

He never wrote, he never phoned, and for several weeks there was only silence.

Amy eventually stopped waiting. She had to get on with her life. She had to start living again.

She had to make plans and build a future for herself…and her unborn baby.

Chapter 2

For once Amy's was sticking to regular office hours. She never normally watched the clock but today, at five, she changed out of her office clothing and scrambled into the casual clothes she'd worn to work that morning.

She'd worn her favourite thick, chunky pullover and a pair of much-loved faded denim jeans. Young girls today were wearing designer labelled stone-washed jeans with a strategically cut slash across the thigh or knee. The ones Amy had on were identical, but it had taken her nearly three years of wear and tear and washing - plus a little boy's sticky fingers - to achieve the same effect.

She looked just as good, if not better than some of the top models who posed for fashion shoots in trendy magazines.

Going down to the lobby Amy handed her pager into reception and Bill, one of the firm's security porters, wouldn't let her go without telling her one of his jokes.

Laughing and smiling in her cheerful way she was about to say goodbye when she felt a hand descend on her shoulder. It surprised her and caught her completely off guard, and her face drained of colour when she saw who it was.

"Great...I thought I'd just missed you," said a deep, masculine voice behind her.

It was Max.

"This isn't happening to me," she thought. *"It can't be happening to me."*

Max took her arm possessively and started pulling her towards the exit.

"You alright, Miss Denver?" Bill stood up from his chair and was about to make a move and come out from behind the protective shield of the reception's Plexiglas screen.

Bill was at the ready and he was willing to defend her.

"I'm fine Bill...thanks," she told the friendly porter in a calm and composed manner.

She could imagine the end result if Bill, aged sixty plus, went head-to-head with Max bouncer-style. She was sure Bill wouldn't come out as the winner.

"I'll see you tomorrow, Bill," she said as reassuringly as she could.

Tender-hearted Bill was left behind looking suspiciously at Max as Amy was frogmarched out of the building and out of sight. Max was pulling her forcibly along beside him and she had no idea where he intended taking her.

"I looked in your office and someone said you had gone. I thought I told you to wait for me. It seems I'm only just in time to catch you before you left," he said angrily.

Max didn't look at all pleased with her.

"You were leaving early weren't you?" he asked.

"Yes," she admitted reluctantly, "I was due some overtime. A few extra hours. I've been working late this week and I thought I'd take them…"

"To avoid seeing me?"

"Yes," she said.

"Well at least she's truthful," he thought. *"Although perhaps a little forthright."*

Amy knew Max was here for a reason. She sensed he was trying to get back into her life…and she was scared.

She didn't want him in her life. Not now. She didn't want him unbalancing the secure world she'd created for Jake and herself.

"Amy we need to talk," he told her bluntly and he grabbed her arm leading her across the road towards the car. "Is there somewhere we can go and have a quick cup of coffee?" he asked.

"No there's nowhere," she told him crossly. "Max it's you who needs to talk…I don't. And right now is not a good time for me. It really isn't. I have to be somewhere in an hour."

She didn't dare tell him she had to collect Jake from day school.

Just when she thought she was getting her life back together Max had shown up and he now wanted something from her.

"I want to talk to you before you have time to do a runner," he told her. "It's taken me quite a while to find you and I'm not taking the risk of having you disappear again."

She hadn't been the one who had disappeared and ended their relationship. It had been Max who had fallen off the face of the earth.

He was the one who hadn't answered his mobile phone when she'd called him, but it was pointless arguing that point with him now.

Max pressed the clicker on the remote control gadget he was holding and automatically the car door opened. He was driving a black Porsche.

It was a rental that had been delivered and dropped off at the law office for his use during his stay in England.

It looked long, sleek and sinister...just like Max.

"Get in," he ordered.

"I'm not getting in there and I'm not going anywhere with you Max," she said holding her ground.

He pulled her roughly against his chest and she could feel his hot breath breathing against her face. He looked down at her from his great height.

"I said get in Amy and I mean it. I won't ask you again...I don't have time to argue with you."

Max held open the passenger door for her and reluctantly she was forced to climb in.

She knew she would have to face him sometime and she supposed it would be better to get it over with sooner than later.

Sinking back into the deep leather seat she took a calming breath.

The Porsche had plenty of leg room which was just as well considering the size of Max. Any vehicle he owned or hired would have to be huge to accommodate his length.

Max walked around the car and got in beside her. Putting the key in the ignition, but not yet starting the motor, he turned and looked at her.

"I need somewhere quiet so we can have a chat and I can explain what's happening. Is there anywhere, in particular, you'd like me to take you?" he asked.

He sounded cool and unruffled and surprisingly relaxed. He sounded like a man who had achieved his goal. He'd gotten what he wanted. But then Max had always been an expert at getting what he wanted.

Five years ago he'd wanted her and for some reason, he wanted her now.

So far he seemed to have achieved his objective.

Sat next to him, Amy felt she was a prisoner in his car until he chose to release her. She'd sworn to herself she wouldn't get involved with him again but it seemed like she was becoming involved.

He was winning.

"I don't mind," she said defeated. "I haven't given it a thought. Wherever you like but I have to be back here in an hour."

"Good...alright then...buckle up...and I promise to have you back here by then," he said.

Max turned the ignition and the car's engine started instantly with a purr.

Amy didn't know anything about cars. She couldn't tell a four-wheel drive from a hatchback, but what she did know was that this one was totally different from her old Ford.

Max adjusted some dials on the dashboard and glanced over at Amy.

"We'll head out of the city and get some fresh air...if that's alright with you?" he said.

"Sure," she said looking at her watch. "Fifty-seven minutes remaining..."

They took the motorway out of the city and Max headed towards the coast.

There seemed no need to speak. The silence wasn't uncomfortable but it helped when he put a CD in and turn the player on.

"So, what's happening in an hour?" he asked.

"Sorry?" she said.

"You said you had to be somewhere."

"Oh yes...I have to meet someone." And that was all she was prepared to tell him.

"Heavy date tonight is it? Lucky man..." he said smiling.

There was a hint of sarcasm in his voice and something else. He thought she had a boyfriend. Well, he could think what he liked. She didn't care.

"No, it's not a boyfriend. I don't have one at the moment," she explained unnecessarily. "And anyway...I learnt my lesson the hard way."

He smiled at her.

"Was I really that bad?" he asked.

Stubbornly she didn't answer him. Instead, she turned her head and looked out of the passenger window at the green fields and cottages they were passing.

When they got off the motorway they drove a few miles along winding roads, passing small villages, heading towards the coastline with its white, sandy beaches and blue sea.

Eventually, they reached a pub perched on a hillside overlooking the sea. Max turned the black Porsche into the car park and pulled on the handbrake.

Amy recognised the place instantly. He'd brought her here one summer, five years ago.

They had been living together in her flat and one weekend their free time had coincided. Hurriedly they had packed a rucksack and had thumbed a lift out of the city until they landed here, at this place.

"Do you remember the day we went surfing here?" he asked.

The beach had been deserted and they'd found a secluded spot where they had stripped and swam naked. How could she possibly forget? And how could she forget their lovemaking among the sand dunes?

"I was young, foolish and..." There was no need for her to say anything more.

"Come on, let's go in and get a coffee," he said before helping her out of the car.

Together they made their way into the pub. It was decorated in a true sea-ferrying tradition. Fishing nets and floats were hung on the walls and an old ship's bell was dangling over the beer pumps at the bar.

Although it was light outside, the interior of the pub was dim with only a few wall lamps lighting the room.

In the summer heat, the coolness of the pub was a haven from the scorching sun, but today, with the cold wind blowing in from the sea, a welcoming log fire was burning in the hearth.

Max and Amy collected their coffees from the bar and made their way to the back of the pub where they wouldn't be troubled by the few customers who had also found their way to this idyllic seaside retreat.

Taking a seat on one of the big oak chairs near a sea-view window, Amy took a quick glance at her watch.

"You have twenty minutes to get your point across," she warned him. "And twenty minutes to get me back to the city."

She then picked up her cup and took a sip of the hot, steamy liquid.

"I need a wife...a temporary bride," he told her.

At that moment she was never more thankful for all the training she'd received in law school on how to stay calm in tricky situations. Unflustered she looked Max squarely in the eyes and calmly placed her cup back on its saucer. She hadn't known what to expect when he'd said he wanted to talk to her but she hadn't anticipated this.

"I need a bride and I'd like you to consider the position," he said coolly.

"I'm sorry...I must be really dense or something."

"No, you heard right. You see...I've got a problem and you're the only woman I know and trust to help me out."

Max hadn't said he loved her and he hadn't gotten down on one knee.

To Amy, it sounded like she was being offered a job.

"I don't get it," she said.

"It's quite simple. I have to stop my brother's wife getting her hands on the family business. The only way to do that is for me to marry...and it has to be soon," he explained.

"And you want me to find someone for you to marry?" she asked.

"No, I don't...I want you...I want you to marry me."

* * * *

Max had said he wanted her to marry him and it felt like he'd just slapped her in the face.

She didn't know how many years she'd waited to hear him say those very words or how many times she'd dreamt of Max coming to find her. She'd even imagined him taking her in his arms and holding her and loving her as he used to. She'd longed to be his once more.

But that hadn't happened then and it wasn't happening now.

Max wasn't telling her he loved her. All he was saying was that he wanted to marry her. And she was scared. She was scared because she knew that whatever Max aimed for he inevitably got.

There was a time when she'd loved him unconditionally with all the innocence and all the passion in her young body. She'd trusted him. And when he'd left her to go back to New York and work in America, he'd badly hurt and wounded her.

Max hadn't been there when she needed him most.

Pregnant, scared and all alone, she'd put on a brave face and she'd shown the rest of the world that she was in control of her emotions and that she could cope. And she had coped.

She'd been resilient and determined and she'd survived. She'd been strong for herself and for her baby.

Ultimately she couldn't blame Max for what she'd chosen to do. He'd made it clear from the start that what they had was a no-ties-relationship. They were both free agents. But she'd been young and vulnerable. With a sheltered upbringing, she'd had no idea of the emotional tangle she was getting into when Max moved into her flat. And when he'd left her to return to America, her world had gone with him.

Now he was back in England and he was asking her to marry him.

"Why don't you marry one of your other women?" she said putting on a brave face. "I'm sure you've got plenty of girlfriends who would be only too please to become Mrs. Jordan."

"That's the problem...I have. And they would be only *too happy* to become my wife. But that's not the sort of wife I'm after. I need someone I can trust and I've always felt I could trust you. That's why I'm here now. I'm here to ask *you* to marry me."

"But I can't marry you," she told him bluntly. "I won't marry you...not like this. It's impossible. I have responsibilities and I have my work. I've built a life here. I just can't leave everything."

"You might not have to leave here. We can play it by ear. We might get away with you living in

England. You could fly to America when we need to be seen as a married couple living together. You can come and see me when we need to make it look official," he explained trying to put over his point.

"Whoa...now hold on a minute. You're going too fast for me. I haven't said I'll marry you," she said putting on the brakes.

"I really need you to do this favour for me Amy and it will only be for six months at the most. I promise. And I'll make it worth your while. You can have a lump sum settlement. It will be more than you'll ever earn at Martin and Campbell," he said with an edge of desperation in his voice.

"Six months? Why six months? No...stop...stop! I don't need to know why. The answer is no Max. *No. No. No.* It's impossible. I can't just quit my job. And there are other things I have to consider. There are other people in my life now."

"What? Who? Do you mean you're living with some guy or are you just dating him?" he said, frustrated that he wasn't making headway.

"No it's nothing like that," Amy said.

"Then what's the problem?"

She wasn't going to tell Max about Jake. She daren't bring Jake's name into the conversation.

"No Max...I'm sorry but we can't," she said trying to sound final.

"Think about it, Amy. We were always good together and we didn't have any major quarrels...except about America." He was not prepared to give up. He was still trying to persuade her to accept his offer.

Amy looked at her watch once more.

"I have to leave now. If you could take me back to the city Max...*please*," she said urgently.

"But this is important..."

"*Nothing* and I mean *nothing* is more important to me than what I now have to do. If you don't mind we have to leave...*now*," she said hoping he would listen to her.

Max was surprised at Amy's determination and assertiveness. Reluctantly he got out of his chair and he led her outside to the car.

"Any particular way home?" he asked coldly and politely. It was almost as if he'd emotionally and physically distanced himself from her.

"The fastest."

Sat in the car, Amy buckled the seatbelt across her shoulder preparing herself for a speedy ride. She wasn't disappointed.

Max always loved fast cars and speed, and today was no exception. He put his foot down on the accelerator and they drove off at a high velocity.

"Where to?" he asked as they were nearing the centre of the city.

"If you could drop me on the corner, near the junction. I don't have far to walk from there." Once again she glanced at her watch. "I ought to be able to make it on time."

"I said - *where to* - not which corner," he said angrily.

"Then if you could take the next right, please. That would be very helpful and thank you."

She'd never been good at making polite conversation with Max. Her parents had raised her to be good-mannered but she'd never been able to mind her p's and q's as far as he was concerned.

With Max, it had always been a full-on passion or outright war.

"Whilst I'm in England I'd like to take you out to dinner. For old time's sake and as a thank you for listening to me this afternoon," he said. He was prepared to try another tactic over dinner.

"I don't think so, Max. It wouldn't be a good idea. It wouldn't do any good to rekindle things between us. I'm prepared to work with you at Martin and Campbell because my boss has more or less ordered me to, but that's it. From nine to five my time is yours. Are we clear on that score?"

She wasn't being railroaded into doing anything she didn't want to do and she was prepared to stand up to Max and tell him so.

"It would be just a meal. Two civilised people making conversation and catching up on each other's lives and..."

"If you could pull into the curb....we're here," she said ignoring his last words.

Amy released the seat belt and didn't wait for Max to open the passenger door.

Quickly she rushed out of the car and went over to the big school gates. They were shut but not locked and she could see him from where she was.

Jake was playing in the schoolyard.

He was sitting on one of the swings looking lost and all alone.

And then Jake looked up and jumped off the swing as he spotted Amy at the gate.

A relieved smile transformed the sorrowful face of the little boy and she was glad she'd decided to hurry to the school and not walk the last couple of streets.

Waving his arms, trying to attract her attention, the small boy ran towards her totally forgetting the backpack he'd left on a bench.

Amy entered through the school gates and bent down opening her arms for Jake to run into.

Just as he reached her he cried, "Mummy...mummy. I've been waiting and waiting."

Amy lifted her son high into her arms, giving him a welcoming squeeze and a kiss.

Jake desperately needed a haircut. His hair was getting far too long and it was constantly falling into his eyes.

"And how has my best boy been today?" she asked smoothing Jake's hair out of his eyes.

But Jake wasn't listening.

He was suspiciously eyeing the man standing beside his mummy.

Amy's eyes darted from Max's dark features to Jake's, and the resemblance between them was so striking it was unmistakable.

For the first time, the man standing beside Amy was looking at the son he never knew existed.

* * * *

Amy stood her ground. She wasn't running scared. Her mother instincts were turned on to maximum-full-force and she was fearlessly looking at Max while guarding Jake.

"Yours?" he asked her through clenched teeth that were firmly gritted together.

"All mine," she told him defiantly and she lifted her chin in the air as if she was daring him to think otherwise.

His face was like a thunder cloud on the point of explosion. He was in a rage and she could see a pulse beating furiously at the side of his jaw. There was no doubt in his mind that he was looking at his own son.

Without any disbelief, he knew that the child before him was his.

Amy clutched Jake closer to her and he squealed and wriggle in her arms.

"Ouch mummy, you're hurting."

She was frightened Max would be tempted to grab Jake and wrestle him from her arms there and then.

Carefully she lowered Jake to the ground where he clung tightly with his tiny four-year-old fingers to her jean-clad legs for security.

Max was looking angrily at her but she wasn't intimidated.

She had a trump card.

She had Jake.

At that moment Jake's teacher looked out of the school building to see how things were and from where Amy was standing she gave the teacher a shaky, but reassuring wave.

"I've been keeping an eye on him. Is everything alright?" The teacher was calling out towards them.

"I'm sorry we're a bit late," Amy called out to Mrs. Jefferies. "Thanks for looking after him."

"Jake hasn't been any trouble...have you, Jake? We'll see you both at school tomorrow. Bright and early."

"Jake, go and say thank you to Mrs. Jefferies and don't forget your backpack. When you come back we'll go home and you can have your tea."

But Jake wasn't letting go of his mummy. He was holding onto her legs and looking daggers at Max.

"Go on. I'll wait here for you," she said, reassuringly giving her son a gentle push towards the bench where he'd left his school books and backpack.

Reluctantly Jake did as he was told and Max seized the moment and caught hold of Amy's arms.

She could feel his fierce grip digging deep into her soft flesh even through her thick, chunky pullover.

"Why haven't you contacted me? In all these years...why have you said nothing?" he asked.

"Not now Max. Not in front of Jake," she implored.

But Jake was out of earshot and there was no danger of him hearing Max's angry words.

"If I hadn't come looking for you, would you have contacted me? Would you have told me about my son?" Max still had hold of her and there was no escape from his fury.

She could see and feel his rage.

"Who knows..." she said hunching her shoulders. "Can't we just leave it for now?"

"And I thought you were the one woman I could trust. My god...I've been a fool."

Jake had thanked his teacher and collected his bag. He was returning to where Amy and Max were still standing.

"Not now Max....not in front of Jake, please," she begged.

"Then when can we talk?" he asked.

She looked at Max and she was fearful Jake would see the hatred and resentment in his father's eyes.

Frustrated, Max let go of her bruised arms and he turned angrily, walking away from her. He walked out through the school gates and he didn't look back.

Amy knew there would be no escaping Max now that he'd found her with his son. And she was right.

Max was leaning casually against the side of the car waiting for them to join him...and he wasn't leaving without them.

* * * *

Max gave Amy and Jake a lift home from the school. There had been no need for her to tell him her new address - he'd known.

She wasn't staying at the flat she'd shared with him all those years ago. She'd managed to get a mortgage and, with some money her parents had left her, she'd put a down payment on a small town house with a garden for herself and Jake.

But somehow Max had found her and he knew where she lived.

Without any hesitation, he'd driven straight to the house.

She shouldn't have been surprised.

Thinking about it now she realised he hadn't been amazed to see her in the office that morning. He'd made a beeline for her as if he'd known where she worked. She should have guessed he would know where she lived.

But he didn't know everything. He hadn't known about Jake.

She'd seen the surprise in his eyes when he'd seen Jake and he couldn't have faked that.

"I won't come in," he told her as he opened the car door for them and let them out. "I've got a meeting with James to review the Diablo lawsuit. But I'll see you this evening. We have to talk. What time does Jake go to bed?"

"About seven," she told him.

There was no avoiding the moment. She would have to face him sometime.

"Then I'll see you about eight. Don't cook...I'll bring dinner. Chinese or Indian?" he asked politely.

"Look, Max..."

"Chinese or Indian?" he asked again.

"Anything...I don't mind," she said, resigned to the fact that she would have to see him.

Max gave Jake a quick rub on the head messing up his hair.

"Bye Jake. See you tomorrow," and then Max looked daggers at Amy. "And I'll see you tonight."

She was left with a gut feeling that her world had just change drastically and nothing would ever be the same again. Max wasn't letting go until he got what he wanted.

Chapter 3

Amy bathed and played with Jake for a while. When she put him to bed with a story he drifted off to sleep without any bother.

Precisely at eight o'clock, she heard the heavy rap of the knocker on the front door. Speedily she rushed downstairs to answer before another pounding could wake Jake. Pulling the door wide open she came face to face with Max.

He'd changed out of the dark, pin-striped suit he'd been wearing that morning. Now he was dressed casually in denim jeans and a blue and white striped shirt with a navy, cashmere sweater that matched the deep blue of his eyes.

A woman couldn't deny him anything with those blue eyes looking at her. He looked casual, relaxed and very sexy...and she was mesmerised.

"Good evening Amy. May I come in?" he asked, and not waiting for an answer he walked straight past her into the hall, tossed the jacket he was carrying onto a nearby chair and went through into the kitchen.

He'd brought a take-away with him and dumping the carrier bags with the boxes of hot food on the worktop, started rummaging in her cupboards and drawers for plates and cutlery.

"Where are the forks?" he asked her while still searching.

He pulled out a drawer and found them before she had time to tell him.

"Get the wine glasses would you? I've brought a couple of bottles of Chardonnay. Yours is the sweet one," he said.

The insufferable man. Who did he think he was?

The place might look a mess and toys were everywhere, but this was her home. Her house. He had no right to be telling her what she should be doing.

Max had set the kitchen table and they were sat down ready to eat.

"So, tell me your story. What's been happening," he said and unceremoniously started eating.

She'd never had the chance to tell Max that when she'd finished her training she'd packed a bag and had followed him to America.

She hadn't told him that when she'd reached New York she'd discovered she was stranded and he was no longer in the city, or that he hadn't answered his mobile phone when she'd had need of him. There had been no way of contacting him.

Her life had been in turmoil and she'd thought it best to put the past behind her and make a new life without him. To be fair Max hadn't known about the baby. If he had, things might have been different.

Amy took a sip of the wine Max had poured for her. It was nice and sweet just the way she liked it. He'd always been a snob when it came to the wine list in restaurants, so it didn't surprise her when he said he'd brought a bottle of sweet wine for her and a dry for himself.

"You first," she said. "What's your story and why are you back in England? You're supposed to be in America."

Max's mouth tightened.

"That was the plan. But things never seem to work out the way I imagine. Look at us for example. I thought you would come to America and we would be together...but...what I thought would happen didn't."

Max took a hefty drink from his wine and refilled his glass. He'd never been a heavy drinker and she didn't imagine he was now, but he seemed to need something to give him a boost.

"Pathetic isn't it?" he said. "I need Dutch courage to say what I have to say."

"And what do you have to say to me Max?" she asked tentatively.

She was listening and she waited patiently until he was ready to begin.

"I need a wife...urgently," he said and he pushed his plate of food away from him as if he'd had enough. "It's difficult to know where to start."

"Then try starting from the beginning," she said with a hint of sarcasm in her voice.

He sat back in his chair and toyed with the stem of his wine glass.

"At the time I'd only just left England and moved back to New York. I was doing a stint with a law firm to gain experience. God, I was young then. Young and full of dreams. Then my father had a stroke. I had no other option but to go home to Waterfront. Waterfront is our family home in the Hamptons. I had to take over the running of our business - Jordan Diamond Empire - which is based in New York. My brother Brad was there to help, but it was hard going at first."

"I didn't know."

"No, you didn't. That was what was so amazing about us. You didn't know who I was and my guess is you still don't."

"Know what?"

"Who I am. To you, I was just a young lawyer studying in England. I was anonymous. I was an unknown entity. You weren't after my fortune or my billions. You hadn't the slightest idea who I was and you still don't know who I am, do you?"

"I don't get it. What are you saying?" she asked.

"Take a look out the window," Max said.

"Why? What for?"

"Humour me," he said firmly.

Amy did what he asked and went over to the window and pulled back the curtains to look out into the dark of the evening. There was a street lamp lit across the road and beneath the bright light of the lamp she could see a long, black limousine.

Standing beside the sleek black car were two men.

Max came to join her at the window and both men put their hands to their gun holsters beneath their jackets.

Max gave a signal that everything was alright and then pulled the curtains together shutting out the night and the sinister view.

"But you're a lawyer," she said, shaking from head to toe from what she'd just witnessed.

She was having difficulty understanding what the two men were doing.

"And why do you have gangsters outside my house? They've got guns. It's not legal."

"They are not gangsters and they're licenced to carry arms. They're my bodyguards. Now they are yours...and Jake's," he explained.

"What? Why?"

"Because I need to know that the two of you are safe at all times."

"But I don't need anyone to look after us," she protested.

She was anxious that things were moving too fast and that she was losing control over what was happening in her life.

Max took hold of her arm and started steering her towards the kitchen door.

"Come on," he said. "Let's leave this and go into the other room."

"Why?"

"So we can sit down and talk some more and so I can tell you what we're going to do."

"I don't need to talk. There's nothing to talk about and there is no '*we*'," she told him.

"Here, take the wine."

He passed her the glass she'd been drinking from and he walked through with her into the lounge carrying the remainder of his wine and the bottle.

Amy picked up a few scattered toys Jake had left lying about on the floor and put them in his toy box before taking a seat on the sofa.

She shouldn't have sat where she did.

Before she realised what was happening Max had joined her on the sofa. He sat back relaxed with his arm running along the back of the sofa behind her.

She could feel his leg pressing against the side of hers and carefully she shifted her position to get away from him.

"You know you never used to do that," he told her teasingly. "I remember there was a time when I couldn't get you off my lap."

"And I remember there was a time when I should have known better. Now, are you going to tell me what all this is about...or not? Especially about those two bouncers outside," she said getting slightly exasperated.

"They are there for your protection. If anyone got wind I was here in England, with you and Jake, the press would have a field day. It's mainly to protect you from the newspaper paparazzi. It's nothing more...and nothing less than that," he explained.

"So why are you in England if it isn't to work on the Diablo case?"

"I've a law office in New York attached to Jordan Diamonds. Any one of the lawyers I employ back home could handle the Diablo case. No, you're right...the case wasn't my main reason for being here," he told her.

"Then what is?"

"You...you're the reason," he confessed.

Max shifted position and sat forward on the sofa resting his arms on his knees. His hand rubbed the back of his neck and she knew what she was about to hear was important.

Max suddenly looked strained and tense.

"I've told someone a lie and I need you to back me up," he explained.

"Then if you've already told a lie how do I know you're telling me the truth now?"

"Because I am...and because there's too much at stake. I'm here because you're the one person I could think of and the one person I know I can trust implicitly. You see, my brother died recently, which means the family business is in jeopardy. There are threats of takeover bids and mergers. It's taken me a couple of months to get things back on track and we're doing okay, only things are on a tight time schedule."

"Who's 'we' and why a tight schedule?" Amy asked a little confused.

"*We* are family and relatives. We import and export diamonds. I never wanted to follow in the family tradition and join the diamond side of the business, but circumstances have now dictated otherwise. As my father's heir, I have a duty to uphold."

"Diamonds...but you're a lawyer," Amy said, shocked at this latest piece of information.

"I am, and I handle most of the administration and legal side of the family's diamond business. I trained as a lawyer but now I seldom enter a court room. I mainly delegate."

"Diamonds and not law?" she asked slightly puzzled.

"Yes. The deal I made with my father was that I'd go to Harvard University and study law. After I qualified and gained a law degree I'd come back and work for the firm."

"In a law firm?" she enquired.

"No...a diamond company. We buy and sell uncut diamonds on the open market. We also design and make our own jewellery."

"I still don't get it," she told him confused.

"Because of my legal training, I tend to cover most of the legal paperwork. Patents and copyrights...that sort of thing. It's an ideal way to combine both my interests, diamonds and commercial law. That's one of the reason's I'm here today," Max told her.

"The Diablo case?"

"Yes."

"And the other reason?" she asked.

"We'll get to the other reason in a moment. My brother died recently and I had to take over his workload and to return to our family home, Waterfront. My family needed support. My father retired when he had a stroke and the company, without my brother's input, had to reshuffle management responsibilities. I now have Jordan Diamonds on my plate full-time. I always knew what my destiny would be from the time I was Jake's age and, as head of a diamond company, you don't have the luxury to do what you like. I can only say that playing lawyer has been fun for a while." There was the sound of regret and disappointment in his voice which he'd hoped to conceal, but Amy heard his loss and sorrow.

"Now I know you're lying to me Max. You never played at being a lawyer. You always took your work very seriously. I've never known anyone more dedicated or more suited to the legal profession. I lost track of the number of nights you came home late because you were burning the midnight oil over legal documents. You were always busy fighting someone's case for them."

She didn't believe him and she wouldn't believe him. The Max she knew had never *'played'* at being a lawyer.

"Those days have gone Amy. My responsibilities are now to my employees and to the business. I can't just drop everything because I have the urge to play saviour."

She'd had enough of him talking as though he'd turned his back on the profession he loved. The Max she knew lived and breathed law. It was in his blood.

"I'm going to get a coffee. Do you want one?" she asked.

She wasn't going to sit here on the sofa and argue with him. She couldn't believe Max would want to sacrifice his law work willingly.

He followed her back into the kitchen and sat at the sturdy, wooden table and watched her as she wandered about the kitchen preparing their coffee. The percolator was on and she began collecting mugs.

"This afternoon I've been busy and I've done a lot of thinking," he told her.

"About what?" she asked.

"About us. I've come to the conclusion that the best solution would be if you and Jake were to move back to America and lived with me." He said it as if it were the most natural thing in the world for them to do.

The empty mug she was holding crashed to the floor shattering into fragments at her feet.

"Mind the pieces," he told her.

He began picking up the scattered bits of broken bone china and placing them in the bin.

"Jake has nothing to do with you and I'm not uprooting him on a whim because you're in trouble," she said, still shaking slightly.

She wasn't going to let Jake leave his day school. He was enrolled at a local primary school which he was due to start soon. The school catchment area where they lived was good, and she and Jake were very happy where they were. No...they couldn't move to America. She wouldn't move.

"He's mine," Max said. "This afternoon I've had you investigated and the birth certificate declares me as being Jake's father. Amy, you've made me miss four years of my son's life. You've kept him a secret from me."

"No, I didn't," she said. "You could have found us if you'd looked."

"Well, you didn't contact me to tell me about him. You've had Jake for four years. Is six months too much for me to ask? I'd like to get to know my own son and catch up on the things we've missed? Can't you at least give me six months of your time?"

"That's the second time you've mentioned six months. What's it all about Max? When I saw you in the office you knew I'd be there working for Martin and Campbell...didn't you? You knew where you could find me."

"Yes, I knew. It took me a while to track you down. The trail went cold at the rented flat we shared together but I found you through your law degree. You have to register if you practice and you were practicing. You were working for James and that was how I found you."

"And you weren't at the office just for the Diablo case were you?" she said, looking him squarely in the eye.

"No. As I said, I could have got someone from my law team to stand in for me. I was there to get to you. At first, I was going to take it slowly. Persuade you gradually, but it's all backfired since I've seen Jake. I didn't know about Jake." Max looked wounded and devastated when he spoke of his son and the loss of their time together.

"Then why? What is it you want from me? You've told me about your family and friends...why the tight time schedule and why do you need to be married?" she asked.

"Leave the coffee for now and come and take a seat."

They were both sat at the big wooden table and as he looked across at her, he rubbed his hands across his tired eyes.

"When my father had a stroke he divided the company between my twin brother, the family and me. Brad and I each had forty per cent and the remaining twenty was held by my relatives...but there were conditions attached. Brad was happy to look after the customer side of the business and I handled all the admin, banking and paperwork. When Brad died, even though he and his wife were on the point of getting a divorce because of her extramarital affairs, all of Brad's estate went to his widow."

"And what does that have to do with you marrying me?" she asked him.

Amy was still wondering why Max had suddenly reappeared in her life having not been in contact for more than four years.

"One of the conditions of inheriting the business is that I have to marry and stay married before I'm thirty. If I don't, two per cent of my share in the company is distributed amongst my relatives, leaving my brother's wife with a forty per cent majority until she dies or remarries," he explained.

"And?"

"All Stephanie has to do is to wait and buy any shares that come onto the open market to increase her majority. If I don't marry she automatically has the majority vote of forty per cent and she can sell Jordan Diamonds to another company. She's planning to merge with her brother's company, Stone Diamonds."

"Wow," Amy said, genuinely shocked.

"If Stephanie is in the driving seat, the Jordan Diamond Empire as we know it would fold, and thousands would be unemployed. I can't let that happen. As much as I'd like to wash my hand of the whole business I can't. My workforce is my family."

Amy realised that to Max, the very thought of Stephanie taking over the family business was unbearable. Everything his father and family had worked for and achieved would be gone.

He got off his chair and poured two mugs of hot, black coffee and passed one to Amy.

"It all sounds very complicated," she said. "Why choose me? I'm sure you know lots of women who are in a better position to help you. And you've probably had lots of girlfriends since we split."

"I undoubtedly have but for some reason, they haven't worked out."

He took a sip of his steaming coffee and put his mug on the table.

"And I'm sure that if you asked one of them to be your wife they would jump at the chance," she said suggestively.

"Aah, that's the problem. I don't want to marry any of them and I don't think I could live with any of them on a daily basis...long-term or short-term. There's a difference between seeing someone for dinner and living with someone as husband and wife. This marriage has to appear to the world to be real. I've many enemies and if anyone got wind the marriage was a lie, they could contest it and my shares would automatically be redistributed. Amy, I don't think you realise what's at stake here," he said desperately trying to get her to understand his situation.

"I probably don't understand. Your world doesn't have anything to do with mine. I don't know the first thing about shares and diamonds, but if you'd asked me for help about choosing washing-up liquid or nappies I'm an expert. But marriage because of mergers...I'm sorry Max but I can't help you. And it would be too disruptive for us." She couldn't sacrifice Jake's wellbeing for Max's wishes.

"Please Amy...it would solve a lot of my problems."

She'd never heard Max ask for something in such a way before. He was almost pleading. But she was determined she wasn't falling into the same trap again. She wasn't going to let him hurt her like she'd been hurt before.

Max had always had the power to make her want him and make her do the things he wanted her to do. With his good looks, charm and sex appeal Max could achieve most things, but underneath his charisma and attraction, he was ruthless.

He knew how to get what he wanted and for some reason, she was terrified.

She was terrified because he wanted her.

He wanted her as a weapon against Stephanie and now he wanted...Jake.

She'd believed that Jake was her secret and Max couldn't get to them, but she was wrong.

"Jake has school and my work is here," she argued logically. "We can't just move to America for six months and then move back. You don't know how hard it's been for Jake and I to build a life here. No...the whole idea is impossible."

"Anything's possible if you want it badly enough," he told her. And it was like a dark cloud had suddenly descended on him.

"You have no right to ask me to drop everything. No...we can't do it. We can't go to America," she said adamantly.

"Listen, Amy...if this is the way you're playing the game you leave me no alternative but to consider taking you to court and filing a suit for custody of Jake. And let me warn you I can get my son any time I like. Make no mistake about that. I can get Jake with or without you and also with or without the court's permission."

This was a side of Max she'd never seen before and it scared her.

Max walked over to the window and looked out. He waved at the two men standing beside the limousine. His message was clear and it was a part of his character that was unknown to her. He wasn't just threatening her with legal action, he was threatening her with much, much more and she knew he meant what he was saying.

All her fighting instincts were coming into action and she was prepared to do battle. But she knew, somehow, she would lose any battle she fought with Max.

"I never thought I'd have cause to say it and I never thought I would, but I hate you Max Jordan. I wish I'd never met you and if you think you can use my son against me I'll make you regret the day you came looking for me. You might make me your wife and we might be married but you'll never have me," she said trying to hold back the tears.

Amy was on the point of telling Max he could go to hell when a little voice cried out from the top of the stairs.

"Mummy...mummy."

Instantly she was alert and ran to see what had disturbed Jake from his sleep.

"Shh Jake...go back to bed. I'll be up shortly to tuck you into bed again," Amy said gently.

"I want a drink mummy," Jake said.

"Alright...one moment and I'll fetch you some milk."

She looked at Max who had joined her in the hall. He stood leaning against the stairs banister.

"I have to see to Jake," she told him.

"I know...but don't think I've finished with you. I'll wait here until you're done. We have to get this sorted one way or another and it has to be tonight. I'm flying back to America tomorrow."

Amy fixed a beaker of warm milk and was about to take it upstairs to Jake. Instead, she passed the milk to Max.

"Here you do it. If we're going to play happy families then we're doing it my way. You see to your son," she said with just a hint of anger in her voice.

"Shouldn't we leave this for another time? I'm not sure how he's going to respond, having me here," Max said hesitantly.

"Jake will be fine...but the sooner you get used to your new role the better." Amy was playing him at his own game.

Max took the offered beaker and went upstairs to his son's bedroom. He found Jake sitting up in bed amongst his soft toys waiting for his drink. Amy followed Max into the room. She wasn't sure how Jake and Max were going to react together and she waited to see what happened.

"You're him aren't you?" Jake was looking at Max and pointing to a framed photograph on the bedside table.

Max handed the milk to Jake and picked up the picture.

"Looks like it. It was taken when your mum and I were at the seaside together," Max said.

It was a snapshot of Amy and Max on a beach.

The day had been spent windsurfing with some friends and someone had captured a photo of the two of them together. It was the only photograph she had of Max.

"Mummy say's it's my daddy," Jake said innocently.

"Does she?" Max raised an eyebrow amazed that Jake had been told anything about him.

"Are you my daddy?"

Amy sat on the bed and brushed Jake's hair from his eyes. She remembered how Max had stood at the window downstairs, threatening to take Jake from her. She was so tempted to tell Jake a lie.

"It's your daddy Jake...and sometime soon we're going to live with him for a while."

Amy wasn't looking at her son. She was looking up at Max, assessing his reaction.

Jake gave Max an intense examination from top to toe and then looked at Amy.

"You mean to live with my daddy properly; just like my friend Hector at school, who lives with his mummy and daddy?"

"Yes," Max said, "Properly...if that's alright with you and your mum."

"It's alright," he said. It was a child's simply answer to an adult's complex question.

"And now it's time for you to be asleep." Amy gave Jake a good-night kiss and switched off the bedroom light, leaving the door slightly ajar. "We'll talk about this tomorrow."

Downstairs Max was pulling his jacket on. He was about to leave.

"Thank you for telling Jake the truth. For telling him I'm his father."

"Max...right now I love our son more than I hate you. The only thing I would gain by telling Jake you're not his father would be the satisfaction of knowing I hurt you. I would never lie to my son and I would never knowingly hurt him."

"We've got plenty of time to sort things out," he said as he turned to leave.

"No, we haven't Max. And there's nothing to sort out...*this is business* and you've got six months of my time. It's a fixed term contract and the clock is ticking."

.

Chapter 4

One week later Max was leaving England bound for America in his private jet and he was taking Amy and Jake with him.

At some point during the past week - in his usual overbearing manner - he'd made the decision that it was best for all concerned if Amy and Jake relocated to America immediately. America was where the Jordan Diamond Empire was based and it was where Waterfront, the Jordan ancestral pile, was situated. He thought it would be best if they all moved to America and showed a united front on his home turf.

"It will look better if we're together as a family in the Hamptons," he'd said.

Amy disagreed and reasoned adamantly against his theory. She'd suggested she and Jake should stay in England and he could visit them whenever he needed to maintain the illusion of a happy family. But her arguments had fallen on deaf ears.

"No," he'd said almost angrily. "We have to been seen to be living together as a couple. Stephanie will have less reason to suspect our marriage is not what it is if we're living under the same roof. I have to keep her from getting her hands on the family business."

Max was accustomed to being in charge of everything that affected him directly or indirectly, and this situation with Stephanie and the Jordan shares was a state of affairs he had no control over.

He was angry, frustrated and annoyed because he was asking Amy to uproot herself causing disruption to her life and Jake's. He disliked the feeling of being indebted to her.

Amy had passionately and vehemently protested concerning her move to America and he'd ignored all her objections. They had gone unheeded.

She'd said she had too much to lose if she went to America. There was her job to consider, Jakes school and her network of friends. She'd told him over and over she couldn't leave and wouldn't leave...but she should have saved her breath. He hadn't listened.

His decision had been made and it was final. They were all moving to America.

Amy spent a long and traumatic week packing and preparing for the journey. There had been limitations to what could be taken on the flight. She could take only hand luggage on board the plane and she'd been warned to bring only the absolute essentials. He told her that the rest of her precious possessions had to be left behind. And surprisingly she'd obeyed his instructions.

Amy was relocating to America because he'd insisted that she should, but eventually, it was agreed it was the most practical solution for them all.

He began organising the move without her knowledge and at some point, he contacted James at Martin and Campbell and fixed an indefinite leave of absence for her. He'd arranged to keep her job open should she want to return.

Everything had been organised.

She had no idea how he'd managed it but she voiced her suspicions, asking if it had something to do with the percentage of law fees Jordon Diamond Empire was prepared to pay Martin and Campbell for her services. She was right of course. Martin and Campbell were more than happy with the money coming their way.

Max had also switched Jake's school and had enrolled him at a private day school in the Hamptons. Everything had been thought of; and during the past week, he'd been planning and systematically re-arranged Amy's life.

Because they were to be away from England for six months, he'd also made the decision that everything concerning the townhouse had to be switched off, locked and closed until further notice.

Again Amy had argued constantly saying he didn't have the authority or the right to get involved with her life, but everything she'd said went unheeded.

He'd made all the decisions for her and when he'd asked her to sign some papers he put in front of her, she had. She didn't have the energy to fight him any longer. Things had been taken out of her hands and she no longer had total control over what was happening.

He'd won. She was coming with him. But he wondered if he would at some point in the future, be paying dearly for his high handedness now.

Preparing to fly to America, Max had been standing outside Amy's house beside a long, black limousine. He was waiting to take them to the airport, but first, he told Amy they would be stopping off somewhere.

He hadn't said what he intended to do or where he was taking them. He just packed Amy and Jake unceremoniously into the waiting limo and they had driven into the city to an old, regal, stone building which was the city's main registry office.

When Amy saw where they were she looked astounded and anxious.

"Why are we here?" she asked. She was staring at him in amazement and horror.

"We're here to get married," he told her. "Sooner or later we'll have to get married and it might as well be now. It will save a lot of hassle. If the deed has already been done before we reach America it less likely to cause problems."

"But you can't just marry me on the spur of the moment." Panic was in her eyes. "You...we...we have to have a marriage licence and the bans have to be read and all that sort of thing."

Amy looked unnerved by what he was proposing and seemed to be frantically trying to think of a reason to postpone the event.

It was clear she was worried. The reality of what was about to happen was beginning to sink in. This was the point of no return.

"That's all been taken care of," he told her, trying to reassure. "I managed to get hold of copies of all the necessary documents in order to get a marriage licence."

Before Amy realise what was happening, Max ushered Amy and Jake from the limo and steered them towards the solid, stone steps of the old registry office. Once outside the large entrance doorway to the office, Amy began protesting, practically begging him to postpone the wedding, but he wasn't listening.

"The sooner we're married the better," he told her.

"Can't it wait? Surely the urgency isn't so great that we have to marry today. What's the rush? It can't be because you *want* me. Not in *that* way."

"If you only knew," he whispered beneath his breath.

Max was feeling anything but distant towards the woman at his side. He still desired her and her closeness could always stir his blood. Who wouldn't want Amy? She was one of the most beautiful, desirable women he'd ever known. But he knew he had to build a barrier against her. He had to keep his distance...for her sake.

Seeing her again, he'd felt the old attraction he'd once had for her rearing its head.

Amy was a very striking woman and he was very much a man. What man could resist her?

Ever since they had met, there had always been a fierce attraction between them and during their years apart, it hadn't vanished. He only had to look at her to still want her. And there was absolutely no doubt in his mind that he still wanted and needed her.

He liked the way she moved. The gentle sway of her hips. The way she flicked her hair when she was nervous or the slow sensual smile that framed her lips and then crept to her eyes. He'd always been fascinated with her body. The smell and the feel of her. But mostly he'd liked her yielding softness as he'd taken what she'd unconditionally offered, night after heated night, in her bed.

Just the thought of making love was stirring his blood and he hadn't even touched her...yet.

If he was going to win her back into his life, he had to keep himself aloof and detached. For now at least.

If he got too close and pressured her into a relationship he realised he could scare her off.

She'd only agreed to this scheme because he'd threatened to take Jake from her.

He had to play the waiting game...but not now. Not today. Today he was rushing her to the altar and there would be no turning back.

* * * *

When the three of them passed through the grand marble archway entrance, Amy felt as if they had left the world she knew behind. And fleetingly she wondered what would be on the other side of that arch waiting for them when they returned.

She knew that somewhere out there was their unknown future. But she didn't know if that future would be a future she and Max could share together.

As luck would have it, she was wearing an elegant combination. A designer dress and jacket, and a pearl necklace which had belonged to her mother. The dress was made from soft, pale linen and it was a slightly darker shade of cream that matched the colour of the pearls.

If she'd been told she was going to her own wedding she would have liked to have had the opportunity to have worn something special for the occasion, but it wasn't to be. And true to form, Max hadn't even considered her wishes. It was clear he hadn't thought she would want to wear something special to suit the occasion.

Dressed in his dark grey, three-piece suit Max looked, as he always did, distinguished and handsome, but in a way he was different. Today he was a man on a mission and a force to be reckoned with.

Whereas before - when they had lived together - she would have dared to run her hands lovingly through his thick, dark hair and kissed him passionately on the lips, today, the powerful, billionaire, mogul figure before her had a "hands off" sign written all over him.

Amy looked at Max and even though she hated him for what he was making her do...she still felt the attraction towards him. The chemistry between them was still bubbling beneath the surface and with just one look he could make her want him.

But she couldn't want him and she wouldn't let herself need him as she had before.

Max, Amy and Jake made their way to the Grand Chamber where the ceremony was to take place.

Cathy Moore and James Martin, who Amy considered very good friends, were already in the large, tall entranceway waiting for the wedding party to arrive.

"Good of you to be here," said Max. He gave Cathy a welcoming kiss and shook James firmly by the hand.

"My pleasure," James said. "It's not every day one has the chance to give such a beautiful woman away."

"I've asked James and Cathy to be our witnesses. And James has kindly offered to give you away," explained Max.

Amy looked shyly and her friends wondering what they must be thinking about the whole situation. She'd never previously mentioned Max to either of them before and here she was, on the point of marrying him, just one week after he'd come back into her life.

They must think she was crazy. And she must be.

She knew Max wasn't marrying her for love or because he couldn't live without her. He was marrying her to keep Stephanie from getting her hands on the Jordan Empire.

"We'll see you inside," Max said to Amy and James.

Then Max steered Jake and Cathy into the inner sanctum of the registry office where he would be waiting for his bride-to-be to join him.

Composing herself Amy was about to join Max for the ceremony when James squeezed her hand tightly.

"Relax," he said. "You're as stiff as a board."

He placed his hands on her shoulders and soothingly he began massaging the back of her neck trying to ease the tenseness out of her muscles.

Slowly she started to relax. Her tension and nervousness began to lessen.

Amy looked at James and she suddenly realised that it could have been James and not Max who she was about to marry.

James had asked her out on a date many times, but she'd always refused. Briefly, she wondered if she was making the right decision...but she knew the decision wasn't hers to make.

She'd always loved Max...even when she'd hated him there had always been love between the two of them.

"Well?" said James with deep concern in his eyes. "You look anything but the happy bride. Are you sure this is what you want? There's still time to change your mind."

"It has to be this way, James. There's no other way," she said, attempting to remain calm.

"Amy, of course, there are other ways. If you need a father for Jake...you could marry me," he said seriously.

"James, you don't understand..." And at that moment the heavy, oak doors to the Grand Chamber were opened.

The music started and the ceremony began and there was no chance to explain. There was no turning back and as she walked towards Max and saw their son standing beside his father, she knew the choice she was making was the right one, even if it hurt her to do so.

She had to marry Max.

Max wanted to present his bride to his family, friends and the world as a *fait accompli*. No one was to question his judgement and his word was to be final. And then before she realized what was happening Max was slipping the silver wedding band over her finger.

"I do..."

With those simple words, she was tied to him.

They were married. They were man and wife.

She looked up into his eyes and felt captured. There would be no escape. She was bound to him and she could see in his eyes that he wouldn't be letting her go.

The wedding party was on the point of leaving the registry office when they were surrounded by hordes of paparazzi vying with one another to get the best picture. The press had been ready and waiting outside.

Somewhere along the line, there had been a leak. The world knew Max Jordan, the diamond billionaire, jet-setting mega-mogul, was getting married and the reporters had been waiting to pounce and pursue them to the airport.

Without delay, Max and Amy said a quick goodbye to James and Cathy and promised to stay in contact. Then the newly-formed Jordan family clambered into the waiting limousine and headed straight for the airport.

It was only after the wedding ceremony was over, and after they had been officially declared man and wife that Amy remembered to ask Max what the legal papers she had signed yesterday were about.

"They were your prenuptial agreement," he told her, straightening his tie.

"But I haven't read them," she said with concern in her voice.

"Then you should have." He saw the fear on her face and put her out of her misery. "Don't worry. You haven't signed Jake over to me for money...but you could have. Read before you put your signature on a document." He had reached for her hand and touched the plain silver wedding band he'd placed on her finger. "Especially now you're Mrs. Jordan."

* * * *

Since leaving the registry office earlier that morning, Max had taken Amy on a roller-coaster ride and they hadn't stopped. In record time they had completed the Transatlantic journey to America in the private jet and Jordan security had been there to meet them.

He'd originally intended taking the helicopter from the airport to his home in the Hamptons but thought better of it. It would do Amy and Jake good to see a bit of his homeland and get a feel for his country. There were no rolling hills of the British countryside to be seen here, and there were no high hedges to peer over or winding zigzagging lanes to travel along, but it had its own beauty. The ride in the Cadillac had been on wide, open roads and after sitting on a plane for several hours, the open roads had given a feeling of space and a sense of freedom.

In this country, there was the illusion of no restrictions.

The Cadillac slowed and pulled into the driveway, stopping at a set of heavy, wrought iron gates. The entrance to the house was barred and the place resembled a fortress. Fort Knox couldn't be better guarded. As the CCTV, cameras posted on either side of the gates, turned and honing in on them, a static, crackling sound came from the intercom and someone on the other end of the system muffled something inaudible.

The gates swung open.

Max and his wagon train of security personnel had obviously been recognised because they passed through the barrier without any problems and were now pulling up in front of the house.

When the car pulled in and stopped, Max got out of the Cadillac helped Amy and Jake from the car. The long Transatlantic journey was at an end. They had finally arrived at their destination.

Several whitewashed outbuildings were scattered about the place, but the main house, which was a huge, sprawling building, was situated in cultivated grounds spread out over several acres.

The surrounding green pastures went beyond the formal gardens, extending as far as the eye could see, down towards a sandy beach and the water's edge.

The house itself was comparatively old and built in a sturdy, classic, prairie ranch style. It was tall and solid and had thick, imposing walls with a wide, spacious porch veranda wrapped all the way around. The casement windows were sparkling and shining in the late afternoon sunlight and impressive thick, heavy steps led up to the house.

They had arrived. They were in America and there was no going back.

Max looked around surveying all that was his.

"Welcome to Waterfront. Welcome to my home...or should I say welcome to *our* home." He loosened his tie and with his hands resting on Jake's shoulders, he felt like a man who had everything he wanted. "Waterfront's been our family home for a couple of generations. Recently my parent moved out of the main house and went to live in the beach house which is over there. If you look you can just see the beach house hidden beyond the trees. Can you see it?" he asked.

Beyond a hill crest was a vague shape of a building amongst the trees near the shoreline, and there was a panoramic view of the sea that stretched into the distance. It was the ocean that drew the eyes and the sound of the waves that held the attention.

"Everything's so big...so vast." Amy was looking about her and seemed mesmerised. Her gaze was captured by the amazing views.

"This is home. May I welcome you both to our humble abode?"

Waterfront had an entourage of staff waiting to greet them and at that moment, a man dressed in a servant's livery, came down the steps towards them followed by two large Doberman dogs.

"I'll take the car to the garage, shall I, sir?" he said.

"Thanks, Hal. The luggage bags are in the trunk. They can go to the bedrooms when you're ready," Max replied.

"Right, sir."

Max bent down from his great height and gave the two dogs a scratch behind their ears.

They were wagging their tails with delight at seeing Max as if they were expecting to be taken for a run with the horses. But Max wasn't dressed for riding and, sensing they were going nowhere, the dog took the opportunity to run off and explore the nearby undergrowth.

Max, Amy and Jake stood together watching them romp.

"Can I go and play with them, daddy?" Jake asked.

All three of them were still dressed in the clothes they had worn to the wedding.

Max whistled over his shoulder and the dogs came running back towards the house.

"Not in those clothes you can't." He gentle tweaked Jake's nose.

He could still be unexpectedly surprised and amazed whenever his son - with childlike frankness and without guile - called him daddy.

Max wasn't used to it and however much he tried to keep his feelings in check, he couldn't.

Jake affected him.

He felt a sense of pride whenever he looked at his son.

This son who he hadn't known existed until a short while ago. Jake was his and he'd no regrets concerning that fact.

The only disappointment - if it could be called a disappointment - was the fact that he hadn't known of Jake's existence until recently. He'd missed so much of Jake's childhood and he wasn't sure who was to blame; Amy or himself.

Perhaps he ought to have tried harder to find her after she'd moved from her flat all those years ago. But after he'd returned to America to start his stint with the law firm, all hell had broken out in the Jordan Empire following his father's stroke. It was during that time that he'd lost contact with Amy.

When Max eventually started searching for her and had drawn a blank at her empty flat, he'd thought she'd moved on with her life and with some reluctance he'd done the same.

Now it seems he couldn't have been more wrong.

She had held on to the memory of their time together and Jake was her daily testament and a reminder to that fact.

He could never replace the lost years with his son and he wasn't even going to try, but he was certainly going make up for lost time. Time he hadn't had with Jake...and time he'd spent away from Amy.

They were together now and he was going to do his best to keep it that way. So far he didn't think he was doing too badly. He had brought her to America and she was in his home...which was more than he could have hoped for a week ago.

Standing on the sturdy stone steps of his house, Max looked every inch the man of his domain. And it was all his.

* * * *

Waterfront was opulence on a grand scale. Amy hadn't imagined Max with this sort of wealth or this sort of lifestyle. From the moment she'd stepped out the door this morning she'd been cocooned in luxury.

At the airport, she'd been protected by bodyguards, and on the flight, the stewards had pampered and catered to her every need before she'd even known what she wanted.

It seemed Max hadn't been joking when he'd told her he was worth billions. And the picture she'd had all these years of Max struggling as a lawyer went out the window.

Stood before her was a mega-mogul. Here was a tycoon of epic proportions...and he was a stranger to her. She had never known this man. The Max she'd known and loved was gone and in his place was an unknown entity.

Waterfront screamed money and wealth and that was something she wasn't used to. She also had to remind herself that it was something she wasn't going to let herself get used to.

In six months she was out of here. Whatever happened she was taking Jake with her and she would be leaving America and leaving Max behind.

On the veranda, waiting to greet Max and his family was a barrage of welcoming servants. As Max made his way towards the house and was about to enter he lent towards Amy.

"Sorry about this," he said quietly, whispering in her ear. Then he lifted her high into his arms and carried her over the threshold and into the cool of the house.

Behind them came a roar of applause and cheering from all the staff standing on the veranda or waiting inside the house.

In the large, tiled entrance hallway was an elderly woman wiping her hands on the striped apron she was wearing and she'd clearly been eagerly waiting for the new arrivals to enter.

"Master Max, it's good to have you home again," she said.

Amy saw Max being taken into a warm embrace by the woman.

"And it's good to be home, Hanna. Amy, let me introduce you to Hanna. She's been with the family since my brother and I were babies."

"Aah...poor Master Brad. God rest his soul."

"Are my parent's here?" Max was shrugging off his top coat and passing the coat to Hanna as he spoke.

"Mr. and Mrs. Jordan are in the drawing room, sir."

Amy had forgotten about his parents and she was suddenly brought back to reality. Max had hidden depths and she wondered what other secrets she'd yet to discover.

She hadn't known she would be meeting his parents today and she didn't know how she and Jake would be received. It wasn't every day your son got married and Amy wondered with some trepidation if she would be resented by her new in-laws.

"We'll go straight in and see them," he said leading the way.

The double doors to the drawing room were already open and Amy and Jake had no other option but to follow as Max entered the room.

Sitting in two comfortable armchairs beside the hearth was an elderly gentleman and a beautiful woman of indeterminate age.

The woman's hair was dark and combed back off her face. She was immaculately groomed and dressed. Adorning her ears were two drop diamond earrings and on her hand was a large diamond engagement ring and a wedding band.

Amy thought she was probably in her early fifties but it was the shape of her nose that gave the game away. It was the same nose that Max and Jake shared. The resemblance between them was striking. These two people were unmistakably Max's parents.

As Max walked into the room the couple look up and instantly their eyes moved and rested with amazement on Jake. Suddenly Amy felt an arm circling about her waist.

Max had come to his full six-foot-two inches and he'd put an arm around Amy. He was also pulling Jake to his side. They stood together as a family.

"Father and mother, may I present to you...Amy my bride and Jake my son."

And there was an unmistakable sense of pride to be heard in his voice.

Chapter 5

Max Jordan walked up to his mother's chair, stooped towards her and gave her a kiss on the cheek. Amy could feel the emotion welling in Max and she could see the sudden reaction and excitement in the eyes of his parents.

All their attention was focused on Jake.

Max was claiming Jake as his son and he was waiting for his parent's response.

"Boy-oh-boy-oh-boy," was the exclamation of surprise that came from the elderly gentleman. "What have we here?"

Max's mother, seeing the uncertainty in Amy's eyes, stood up and came towards her.

"Hello, my dear," she said. "We knew something was happening when Max phoned through and told us to open up Waterfront. He gave strict orders to have the house ready for this evening. You see, we don't live very far away. Alexander and I are at the beach house. We knew Max was coming home because we were told he was flying back this afternoon...but we hadn't realised he was bringing a ready-made family with him. We didn't expect this, did we, Alexander?

But it's so lovely to have you all here. Just such a surprise."

Kim Jordan gave her daughter-in-law a warm, welcoming embrace and a kiss on the cheek. Amy hadn't known what to expect when she arrived at Max's home but she hadn't anticipated such a welcome.

Meanwhile, Max had reached down and had taken Jake's hand.

"Come on Jake...come and meet Grandpa Jordan," he said.

Taking his son by the hand, Max led Jake towards Alexander Jordan.

Although Alexander was retired as head of the Jordan Diamond dynasty, he was still a formidable man to contend with. In many ways he was very similar to Max.

Kim gently patted Amy's hand.

"I expect Max hasn't told you a thing about us...has he?" she asked kindly.

Amy shook her head totally overwhelmed by the whole situation.

"No...he hasn't."

"That's to be expected. Even as a boy Max was never a talker." Kim pressed a buzzer near the fire and said, "I'll ring for Hanna and have her bring a fresh pot of tea. Meanwhile, what would you like to know about us? Come and sit down, my dear."

Kim gracefully waved a hand indicating the sofa and Amy went over and sat.

"Please don't bother with the tea. We had plenty to eat and drink on the plane. Jake will be sick if he has any more," Amy said politely.

"Tea...an excellent idea. It's just what we need." Max was totally ignoring Amy wishes. "I'm sure you two ladies have a lot to talk about and a fresh pot of tea is just the thing."

The afternoon passed quickly. Everyone got to know one another and of course, the grandparents were over the moon about Jake. All too soon Kim and Alexander were taking their leave and being driven back to the beach house on the shoreline. And as Amy and Max still stood at the main door waving goodbye to Jake's grandparents, Jake started to yawn and his eyelids began to droop.

Amy picked her son up in her arms.

"If you don't mind, I'd like to put Jake to bed for his afternoon nap," she said.

She had no idea where the bedrooms were or where they would be sleeping that night.

"Hanna can take Jake to his room," Max told her and he took the heavyweight of Jake out of her arms, "Come and meet Hanna. She's about somewhere. Hanna used to be my nanny and now she's going to be looking after you, Jake."

"But my mummy looks after me." The sleepy Jake had mumbled into the lapel of Max's jacket.

"Your Mum is still going to be here for you. But she is going to be very busy looking after me as well. So we thought Hanna could help."

At that moment Hanna appeared with the two Doberman dogs - Daniel and Penny. The dogs came running along the hall. The hall had an imposing, central staircase branching off into two separate wings of the house and there were several tables scattered about the place upon which stood huge colourful porcelain vases filled with massive arrangements of freshly-cut garden flowers.

Seeing the dogs Jake was instantly distracted.

"We don't usually allow the dogs upstairs master Jake, but because you're here, perhaps we'll allow it just this once." Hanna was obviously wise in the ways of children and was becoming a fast friend of her new charge.

There were no arguments from Jake and he went willingly up the stairs with Hanna and the dogs to inspect his new bedroom.

Max and Amy were left together in the large entrance hall. Everyone else had disappeared, and for the first time that day Amy was totally alone with her husband. Max walked towards her and stood towering over her. She had to lift her head to look at him.

"It would seem you're out of a job," he told her. "For the remainder of the afternoon, it appears you're all mine, *Mrs. Jordan*. What would you like to do?" he asked.

Max sounded like a gracious host but Amy wasn't having any of it.

"Firstly, I'm not all yours and secondly I will never be yours. But having said that, I'm prepared to act civilised for Jake's sake and for the sake of your parents. So, what I'd like to do is change out of these clothes, if that's alright with you. I'd then like to see if my son has settled in."

She was still dressed in the soft, cream, linen dress and jacket she'd worn to the wedding ceremony.

"Sure. Of course, it's alright. I'll show you to the bedroom where the luggage's been taken," he said.

Amy followed Max upstairs and he led her into a large suite of rooms. He took her into the master suite where all the rooms oozed opulence and luxury. There was a massive dressing room with a chaise lounge in the corner and they each had their own walk-in wardrobe connected to the en-suite bathroom. But that wasn't what held and captured her gaze causing her to be rooted to the spot.

What had caught Amy's attention was the huge king-sized bed she could see in the next room.

She stood in the doorway not daring to enter.

She hadn't really considered what the sleeping arrangements would be and she certainly hadn't anticipated having to share a bed with Max.

"It's ours, Amy. And if you think we're sleeping separately you can think again. It would give the game away. What did you imagine we would be doing?"

"I don't know what I thought. But I didn't think it would be like this," she said, unsure of how she felt.

"No one...and I mean no one, especially my enemies, can have reason to question the validity of this marriage. If they were to doubt our marriage they would doubt my parental rights to Jake. So you'd better get used to letting everyone know this marriage is real. But don't worry, I won't touch you. It only has to look like a marriage...for six months."

"Can't we sleep in separate rooms? Or separate beds?" she asked.

"The servants would know if we slept separately. And, although I trust them implicitly, I can't take the risk."

She didn't know how she was going to cope sharing a bed with Max. Just being near him was torture, but sleeping with him...she didn't want to be put in that predicament and she didn't want to get involved with him. In fact, she didn't want to get involved with any man.

Aware that Max was physically capable of turning her on sexually, she wasn't going to put herself in the same vulnerable position she'd been in five years ago.

It simply wasn't an option.

She didn't want to become emotionally or physically involved with Max only to lose him again.

Being a single parent had been a hard struggle but she'd learnt that she and Jake could survive without a man in their lives. She knew she could cope. But once this marriage was over, she didn't know how she would survive if her heart was broken once again.

Amy wasn't prepared to be used and discarded and she was determined Max wasn't going to have the chance to destroy her life a second time.

All day Max had been controlling and dishing out his orders and Amy, goaded and driven to a breaking point, could give as good as she got.

"If you lay one finger on me Max Jordan I'll walk out of here and I'll take Jake with me," she said warningly.

She was making a brave stand against him.

"And it works both ways, Amy. Because if you lay one finger on me...I'll take all I can get from you. After all, I'm a man and I still have needs."

She heard the message behind his threat.

"There is no doubt you can arouse me, Max. You always could. But that doesn't mean I want to start from where we left off and begin our affair again."

"Who's talking about an affair? We're married...*Mrs. Jordan*...and we are on our honeymoon." This time there was a flash of desire in his eye as he spoke.

"But it's a marriage on paper only. I'm sure you'll be able to get your needs fulfilled by someone somewhere, but it won't be from me or in my bed."

She thought that Max could look elsewhere and find some available sexy socialite to spend the night with. But it wasn't going to be her.

This bickering wasn't getting them anywhere. They were arguing like children.

"Amy come on. Let's call a truce. At some point, we have to be able to talk about how things are between us. We've got to get along together for Jake's sake. Surely we can at least be friends." Max was trying to appease the situation.

"I don't want to be your friend Max Jordan."

She'd never wanted to be friends with Max. She had wanted more. She had wanted his love. She'd wanted him...all of him. Max stirred her blood too much for friendship.

"I'm not trying to run your life," he told her honestly.

"Well it seems like you are," she said, still not convinced.

"I'm not...I promise," he said. Taking off his jacket he threw it over the back of a chair. "But for now I'll show you where your luggage has been put and after you've changed we'll see the rest of the house. When Jake's had a sleep maybe we can even have a walk in the grounds with the dogs. There's a path that leads through the woods and down to the beach. How does that sound?"

"Fine," she said.

Reluctantly she was agreeing to his suggestions and unwillingly she was prepared to meet him halfway...for Jake's sake.

Max opened the door to the walk-in wardrobe and she saw a long line of elegant dresses and beautiful clothes hanging tidily on the hangers, but her own clothes were nowhere to be seen.

"Hanna must have left someone's things here by mistake," she told him, "These aren't mine."

Then she was amazed as she saw some of her own clothing amongst the range of designer dresses.

"They're all yours," he told her running his hand along a rail of silk blouses. "All the clothes in here are yours and they've not been worn. I've had them shipped in this week from Paris. They ought to be your size."

His eyes raked over her body almost as if he was undressing her and assessing her curves. Amy had gained a few inches around her bust since her pregnancy but it was clear he liked what he saw. He'd always told her that he liked the feel of her body as she melted and squirmed against him.

"If you don't like the clothes, we can send them back and you can choose what you need," he said.

The dresses, shoes and bags were all exquisite and no one in their right mind would want to send them back.

"They're gorgeous Max and you're very generous, but I'm afraid I can't accept," she said.

"You have to wear something. When we left England I told you to bring only the basics."

"But these are too expensive. And I don't expect you to buy clothes for me. I'm not your concubine and in the truest sense of the word, I'm not your wife. You said you needed someone for six months. Ours is a business arrangement...remember?" she said, reminding him of their agreement.

"Then if that's the way you want to see things, let's just say you need something to wear whilst you're here and I'm providing you with a change of...*uniform*?"

Amy felt she'd been put in her place. Max had made a very lavish gesture and she'd behaved badly. She'd more or less thrown the clothes back in his face and he looked anything but happy about the whole situation.

"Now that we've got that sorted, I'll let you get changed and, when you're ready, I'll give you a tour of the house and you can see where you'll be *working* for the next six months."

She looked him straight in the eye. "That's fine by me Max, as long as it's only for the next six months."

Max ran a hand through his dark hair in frustration and, turning away from her, he walked out of the dressing room and into their bedroom next door.

Realising she'd wounded his pride and that she'd overstepped the mark, Amy followed him into the bedroom wanting to make amends. But she realised she'd made a big mistake the moment he turned and walked up to her to face her head-on. Lifting her chin proudly, she'd no option but to look him squarely in the eyes.

"Listen," he warned her.

She could see he was having difficulty controlling his temper and emotions. Then his hands came up and they were gripping her arms crushingly.

"We can make things easy or hard for each other. Which is it to be?" he asked.

"They can't be any harder than you've already made them," she told him defiantly. She was clenching her fingers into fists of frustration. "I'm out of a job and I'm out of my home. You've even threatened to take my child. How much harder can things possibly get?"

She was desperately trying to hold back the tears of emotion that threatened to well up in her eyes.

Max put one of his hands against the curve of her neck. His other hand wound tightly around her waist. He then yanked her brutally hard up against him.

"It can get as hard as this..." he said.

His lips found hers and he plundered her mouth. She felt him roughly forcing her lips apart.

His onslaught was unexpected and it was intense.

She was hit by the provocative fragrance of his cologne as she fought for air and the scent of him was making her senses whirl.

Max had already shed his jacket. His tie had been loosened and she could feel the sensual, silky material of his shirt as she frantically reached for something to hold on to. There was only Max's firm body for her to grasp and he was the only thing from stopping her from falling.

He'd taken control of the moment and the only thing she was aware of was the closeness of his body pressing forcefully against hers.

"Does James Martin kiss you like this...and like this?" he asked her.

His mouth was searching and finding hers again and again. She surfaced for air. Her head was spinning with sensations and emotions she hadn't experienced in years.

"James? What does James have to do with us?" she asked bewildered.

She didn't know why Max should mention James.

"I saw the way you were talking to James at our wedding," he said, searching her eyes for a flicker of emotion.

"Yes, we were talking."

"I didn't like it," he said.

"But we were only talking."

Max cupped her face between his long, powerful fingers. Spreading them out, he moved them capturing her silky-smooth hair in his grip.

"I still didn't like it," he told her almost angrily. "Did he touch you like this? Does James touch you here...and here?"

His hold on her was forceful. Brutal even. And his hands began moving sensually over her body.

Amy was being touched in places no man had been near except Max.

"No Max," she pleaded beseechingly, wondering what was causing him to act in this manner.

"Yes..." he moaned uncaringly against her lips.

"But you're hurting," she cried.

As if realising what he was doing, his cruel harsh hold on her abruptly stopped and then gradually his touch changed. It became softer. His eyes were looking into the wounded, deep dark pools of hers.

With her gaze transfixed on his face, she felt his fingers begin to caress her in an excitingly familiar way. She remembered the feel of him only too well. And slowly his hands began their tender rhythm.

Gently he began kneading her flesh and then he was sliding his hands between the soft silk of her dress, touching the smooth, bare expanse of her exposed skin. His fingers played teasingly with the zip on her dress. Pulling and tugging the dress downwards he let it fall into a pool of silk at her feet.

Unclipping the clasp on her bra, he released the pressure on her breast, freeing them from their confines only to replace the pressure with the exquisite touch of his fingers. Her breasts were bare, exposed, and the long, slender shape of her body was uncovered and revealed for his eyes to see.

"Max," she gasped.

She was shocked at the caress of his hands against her tender, swollen nipples.

Hardly conscious of what was happening, she was being carefully manoeuvred across the room towards the large king-sized bed that was waiting invitingly. The firm mattress pressed against the back of her legs.

She could go no further and there was nowhere to go, except the bed.

Her legs buckled and together they tumbled and lay together on the soft, cushioning quilt of the luxurious eiderdown.

Once more his lips were returning, hungrily seeking and claiming hers. Hurriedly, and consumed with the same intense passion and desire as his, she pulled his shirt away from his trousers matching his urgency and giving kiss for kiss.

She felt a deep uncontrollable shudder run through Max as she caressed him and she had no desire to fight or resist as he forced a leg between hers. In an instant he had fully aroused her. She could feel an all-consuming heat growing between her legs as he plundered her mouth and took what he wanted. Her nipples were hard and swollen and her lips were bruised and tender.

Amy felt completely dishevelled, wanton and very desirable. Max was cupping the fullness of her breasts in his lean, strong hands and whilst covering her mouth to stifle her groans of pleasure, he shifted and rolled, taking her with him.

She was being pushed deeper and deeper, sinking further into the softness of the pillows and cushions beneath them; and together they lay in the heat of their burning bodies.

Then as Max caressed and licked her skin, teasing his moist, hungry lips down passed her taut, ripe breasts towards her navel, she pushed him from her.

It was her turn. She wanted to be in control.

Max was still wearing too much for her liking and slowly, she started to undo the buttons on his shirt. With trembling fingers she released each button, kissing his exposed skin lingeringly. She was playfully delaying the moment until she moved on to the next button. It was a long drawn out seduction which Max was enjoying.

With his shirt finally removed, delicately she ran her fingers through the fine, dark dusting of hairs on his chest.

Letting her hand slip down him, and reaching for the bulge in his pants, she felt his stiffness. He was swollen, ready and waiting to be released.

Amy struggled with the buckle of his belt. Tugging at the zipper she freed him.

"Don't stop," he groaned against her mouth and lips...and she didn't.

They lay skin on skin, totally naked. Their bodies were pressed together. The weight of him on top of her was crushingly hurtful but oh so pleasurable.

Amy was ready for him and she could feel his hardness grinding and throbbing urgently against her.

She had an uncontrollable urge to join as one with him...but she couldn't. Not now...not yet. Abruptly she stopped and pulled away. She wanted him as much as he wanted her but she couldn't go through with it. She was remembering the threat he'd made that he could make things easy or hard for her. And Max was making it hard.

Max, sensing the change in her mood, rolled onto his back pulling her with him.

Amy was now lying on top.

Resting her head against the warmth of his broad chest, she could hear the heavy thud of his heart pounding forcefully in her ear. She was still trembling with pleasure and urgent need of him but their moment of passion had gone. The moment had passed. The mood had been broken.

"I can't," she told him with anguish and agony in her voice. "It wouldn't be right."

Her heavy, laboured breathing matched his.

She knew he was excited and she knew that if he wanted to he could take her forcibly against her will. She was exposed and vulnerable and there would be nothing to stop him from taking her right now and right here if he so wished.

"What is it? What wouldn't be right? And why did you stop?" he asked.

Her cheeks were burning with excitement, but she also felt embarrassed and mortified at what she'd nearly done. How could she have been so reckless?

Amy turned her face away from him keeping herself rigid in his hold. She was resisting the urge to melt and to touch him and caress him as she used to.

Slowly she got off the bed and, seeing a dressing gown draped over a chair, she grabbed it, covering her nakedness. Tying the belt tightly around her waist she thrust her hands deep into the large pockets.

Looking at Max lying naked and still aroused on the bed she felt tempted to stay, but she couldn't. She couldn't let herself be drawn into loving him as she'd before.

"I stopped because I don't mix business with pleasure *Mr. Jordan,* and like you said, I'm business...temporary business....six months, remember?" And she walked out of the room.

Chapter 6

From somewhere in the next room Amy heard the soft click of the bedroom door closing and she knew Max had gone on ahead. He would be waiting for her downstairs.

Having a quick shower and standing in front of the wardrobe she looked longingly at her old denim jeans which she'd found hanging amongst the array of new clothes. She desperately wanted to put them on and wear them. She felt she needed to be in her own clothes and in her own comfort zone. But she couldn't.

Reaching into the wardrobe she took out a pair of designer slacks and a matching mohair sweater which Max had bought and paid for.

'He's won the first round,' she thought. *'But the battle isn't over yet.'*

He was playing havoc with her emotions and she knew that if he made a move she could easily give in to his demands. If she was to survive she would have to stay immune to him.

Even living with Max she was taking a gamble. And if he found out just how much his nearness still had the power to affect her, she would be defenceless against his onslaught.

Dressed in the slacks and sweater, she went through to Jake's bedroom and waited for him to finish his nap before going downstairs with her son.

Spending the afternoon as a family had been good. They had been out in the grounds walking with the dogs and Max had taken them around to the stable block to see the horses.

It was the first time Max and Jake had really had an opportunity to be together as father and son and both of them had enjoyed each other's company. But the shared family moment together had been short-lived.

No sooner had they returned to the house, Max's attention was being sought elsewhere. Word had got out and had reached friends that he was back in the Hamptons and the house phone hadn't stopped ringing. During the evening he was constantly called to the phone.

Having put Jake to bed for the night, Amy and Max were sitting in one of the drawing rooms having a drink before dinner, when the phone rang once more.

"I wonder who it's going to be this time," he said.

He sounded frustrated, and running his hand restlessly through his hair, he walked over to the heavy, oak desk and lifted the receiver.

Amy recognised the tale-tale signs of tiredness.

When they had lived together in her flat, Max had often come home after a hard day in the judicial courts and he looked like he did now...exhausted.

During the past week, he'd had a gruelling schedule. Max had been constantly flying back and forth from America to England on business, and today had evidently been an even longer day. Today they had been married and on the flight to America, while Amy had been relaxing with Jake in the lounge area of the jet, Max had retreated to a corner of the plane and hid behind the screen of his laptop working. He'd been catching up on a backlog of memos and briefs he'd missed.

This afternoon, meeting his parents had been quite an ordeal for them both. They had been constantly on guard not to reveal the true state of their marriage and now, this evening, he was continually called to the phone.

Max looked tired and Amy suspected he was probably suffering from jet lag and only wanted his bed, but she wasn't going to tell him he should go to bed.

If Max went to bed that meant she too would have to retire for the night. So for as long as possible, she was putting off the moment when she would have to share his bed and lie awake for hours beside him.

No! Telling Max to go to bed was not an option.

Max was still on the phone, and on the other end, Amy could hear a voice talking but couldn't quite make out what was being said.

"Yes, come around," Max said to the caller. "We aren't doing anything at the moment and I'm sure Amy would love to meet you. Now is as good a time as any for you two to get to know each other."

The caller said something.

"Great...we'll see you in ten minutes." Max put the phone down and looked at Amy. "Frank's heard I'm back and that I've brought a woman in tow. He's on his way."

Amy raised her eyebrows wondering who Frank was.

"Frank and I go way back. I've known him for years. We went to Harvard together and he's based in our New York practice," Max had answered her unspoken question.

"And he lives near here?"

"No. He lives in Toronto. Why?"

"Toronto..." she was puzzled. "My geography's awful. I thought Toronto was in Canada."

"That's right. It is," he said.

"But I thought you said he would be here in ten minutes."

"He will be. He's taking the jet," Max said in a matter of fact way. "Frank will travel from Toronto to East Hampton Airport by jet and then he'll transfer to the chopper for the short flight to Waterfront."

"Oh well, that explains it." There was a hint of sarcasm in her voice. "Some of us take the bus while others hop on a plane."

"Get used to it Amy. That's the way we do things here," he said. And casually, he shrugged his shoulders.

Amy kept silent not daring to tell Max she had her feet firmly on the ground. She knew that one day soon she and Jake would have to leave the Hamptons and their everyday life would have to return to normal. It would be buses and trains - not jets and planes.

Things were getting too much for her. His friends and the outside world were fast approaching and she had to find some space in which to think and come to terms with what was happening. She had to get out of there.

"Do you mind if I have a look around while I'm waiting?" she asked. "If I'm to do as you say and *get used to it,* I'd better have a look at the house and grow accustomed to the luxuries my husband is providing me with." She didn't wait for an answer.

Amy stood up and walked out of the room.

Half-heartedly she began exploring the downstairs rooms and there were many of them, all very beautifully decorated with spacious, high ceilings and hardwood flooring, but she felt she was missing something. She was missing the homeliness of her small townhouse in London.

Here, there was none of the clutter of scattered toys lying about the rooms and although the kitchen was immaculately clean and equipped with all the latest gadgets, it lacked the comfort of hers.

Finding her way along the maze of corridors Amy eventually came to the grand staircase and started to climb the stairs intending to check on Jake. His room was across the corridor from the master suite and, opening the door carefully, she went in.

Jake had been put to bed several hours ago and it was about time someone looked into his room to make sure he was alright.

Usually, he was quite good at calling out to her during the night if he needed anything, but today hadn't been a normal day for a little boy of nearly five. He had gone to bed exhausted.

Jake was still sleeping securely between the sheets with his favourite stuffed bunny and, because he was still sleeping, Amy carefully woke him and carried him to the bathroom before returning him back to bed.

Curling onto his side he whispered, "nighty-nighty mummy" and fell instantly back into a deep sleep.

Leaving the night-light on and checking to see if the baby monitor was also connected, Amy started tidying some of his clothes and toys away into cupboards.

One of the few things that had been brought from England with them in their hand luggage was the beach photo taken when Amy and Max had been windsurfing. Amy turned the photo on the bedside table so Jake could see something familiar should he waken during the night.

She was about to leave the room and return to Max when she heard the distant hum of helicopter rotor blades as a chopper drew near to the house.

Going over to the large casement window Amy pulled back the curtains and looked outside into the darkness of the night. Sure enough, in the distance some way from the house and the stable block, a chopper was coming into land on the floodlit helipad.

She'd seen the round, white slab of concrete earlier that day but she hadn't realised exactly what its purpose was until now.

Now she knew...and Frank was obviously arriving.

The reality of the world she was now a part of was beginning to hit home, but she still couldn't get used to the idea that it was the norm to hop on a plane to visit a friend. In her circle of friends that just didn't happen.

Looking at the sleeping Jake and checking the baby intercom once more, Amy went back downstairs to welcome their guest.

Reaching the hall she heard the murmur of muffled voices coming from the drawing room.

Max was sitting in one of the big, leather armchairs and across from him was a man about the same age. They were deep in conversation.

Amy stood in the doorway waiting for them to notice her and, eventually, when Max looked up he saw her.

Max got out of his chair and came across the room to meet her.

"Come and say hello to Frank," he said putting an arm possessively around her waist and steering her towards Frank.

"Did I tell you Frank and I used to be at university together? Frank was the one who studied and I was the one who fooled around...which is probably why he's such a brilliant lawyer and everyone wants his services," Max said pleasantly.

Frank threw back his head and laughed loudly before saying, "I wish that were true. It's Max who's the brilliant one. He always wins his court cases. I've never known him to lose."

Frank shook hands with Amy and she liked the way he smiled openly at her.

"It's nice to meet one of Max's friends...at last," she said.

"Oh, I'm only Max's friend when he wants to take time off work or he needs someone to cover for him. He's seldom away from the job, but now that you're here I'm sure things will change. News travels fast and when everyone hears Max is back in the Hamptons, I expect you'll have an onslaught of social callers. Especially when they discover he's just got married. They will all want to come and visit the happy couple."

Amy looked up at Max adoringly as if she worshipped the ground he walked on.

"And we'll be happy to see them. Won't we darling?" she said.

But Max saw through her ploy and he knew she would scratch his eyes out if he gave her the chance. Still holding her tightly to his side, she felt him give her a warning squeeze.

"Behave," he whispered sternly in her ear and then returned the falsely adoring look.

She had to remember her marriage to Max was a pretence, a façade. They were anything but a happy couple. And if any of his friends were to call unexpectedly at the house they would be in for a big surprise. Max had warned her no one was to know their marriage was in name only and it seemed Frank was to be deceived as well.

"May I congratulate the bride?" Frank said, and without waiting for permission he lent forward and gave Amy a kiss on her cheek.

There was a sudden instant tension in Max. His face was smooth and unreadable but she knew he was making a statement when she felt him stiffen as he pulled her closer to his body.

"At first Amy wouldn't have me," Max revealed to Frank quite openly. "She refused my proposal. So I feel that it is I who ought to be congratulated. I'm the lucky one."

Frank reached out and shook Max by the hand.

"Of course you're a lucky guy, Max. And you both have my best wishes. You only have to look at Amy to see your good fortune. I hope your marriage together is a long and happy one."

"It will be," and before she realised what Max meant to do, he'd swooped down and was forcefully kissing her tender lips.

Max kissed her long and hard on lips that were still sore and swollen from his onslaught earlier in their bedroom. He was possessively claiming her as his and he was doing it in front of Frank.

There was to be no doubt. It seemed that Frank and the world was to know that she belonged to Max.

"I've come to take you both out to dinner," Frank told them. "We're going to New York City. I've phoned around our circle of friends and we're making it a wedding dinner on the *River Boat*. Afterwards, we can all go on to a club for some dancing if you like."

For some reason, Frank had come to Waterfront to persuade the newlyweds to go out for the evening.

"What? Why? And who have you asked?" Max sounded reluctant to leave the house.

He'd had a gruelling week and he only wanted his bed but Frank was insisting on giving them a proper wedding dinner. Frank was also adamant that it was only right and fitting that Max should take his new bride out to celebrate.

"Some of our guy's from legal and their wives have promised to be there," Frank explained.

"We can't go," Amy said. She was concerned about leaving Jake but she was also concerned that Max was exhausted. "It's Jake's first night here. He could wake and if we're not here..."

"I'll go and find Hanna and ask her to keep an eye on Jake while we're out," Max said.

It seemed Max had made a decision to go along with Frank's plans for the evening.

"We'll only be gone a couple of hours at the most," he told her.

"Jake's never been left on his own before," she warned. She was still reluctant to leave.

"He'll be alright and he knows he's safe. Now is there anything else you need to do before we leave?" Max thrust his hands deep into his trouser pockets. He was looking at Amy and she knew by the look on his face she had no option but to comply.

"I'll go and change," she told the two men in a matter of fact way. "And as I've never been to New York City before and I'm not familiar with the restaurant we're going to, one of you will need to advise me. What do I wear? Casual or formal?"

"Anything will do," Max and Frank both said in unison.

"Typical men."

Frank was pleased that the ball was rolling and that Max and Amy had agreed to dine out.

Somewhere among the many dresses that Max had bought, she thought there ought to be at least one dress that was suitable for the occasion.

She went to get dressed and by the time she was ready Max had spoken to Hanna about keeping an eye on Jake and he was now waiting for her outside on the wide veranda with Frank.

She could see from the admiring glances that came from the two men that she looked stunning. Her height was accentuated by the heels she was wearing and the long, but simple, silk, cream, sheath dress with sparkling diamante sequins showed her figure off to perfection.

"You can't walk anywhere in those high heels," Max said dampening her joy.

"Of course I can," she protested.

"Stay here with Frank and I'll get the car," he told her abruptly.

It was almost as if he was irritated about something.

"I'll go and change," she offered.

"No, don't bother. I won't be long." Gruffly he walked off to where the cars were housed in a renovated outbuilding.

Whilst Max had gone to collect the car Amy and Frank stood waiting on the veranda.

There was a brief awkward moment when she wondered if she should be the one to start a conversation but she needn't have worried.

"So, you're the one Max has been endlessly searching for and it seems, at last, he's found," he said.

Frank was leaning casually against one of the pillars supporting the veranda.

"I don't know what you mean," Amy said.

She didn't know if he was being serious or sarcastic.

"Max said he'd met someone while he was in England and was sort of in a relationship. I thought he was joking at first but it seems I was wrong. And I thought I knew everything there was to know about Max and his women."

His women.

Max obviously had women in the past and he would probably have plenty of them in the future, but right now she and Jake were in his life and if she was to make it seem they were together as a family, she had better start right now.

"We met a few years ago when he was studying commercial law," she explained.

She hoped she wasn't about to say something that would give the game away. "Neither of us wanted to commit to a long-term relationship at the time. The circumstances weren't right. But now..."

She purposely didn't finish what she was saying and she thought she'd leave Frank to make of her unsaid words whatever he liked.

"I knew he must have met someone in England. When he came back to the US he was a changed man," Frank said.

Their conversation was cut short and they didn't have time to talk any further. Max and a chauffeur had pulled up in front of the house. It was the signal for Amy and Frank to get into the car and ride the short distance to the helipad. Frank opened the door for Amy and she climbed into the back seat with Max.

On the way to the helicopter, Max handed her a package.

"Open it," he told her. And when she did, a delicate, shimmering diamond necklace with a bracelet and earring set was revealed.

She thought that they must be worth millions. And she was right.

Amy looked at Max confused. She wondered why she was being given the diamonds.

"They're yours," he said.

"But I can't wear these," she protested. "They're far too valuable for me to wear."

Amy felt for the plain silver wedding band on her finger and would have preferred to have worn only her wedding ring if it had been given with love.

"My business is the diamond trade and if you don't wear diamonds tonight people will start to think I'm about to become bankrupt," he explained.

She was reluctant to take anything so obviously expensive from him. Then Max delivered a blow she wasn't expecting.

"You're wearing them. And if that's a problem...think of it as promoting *our business* and consider them part of the uniform."

How could she have forgotten their argument about her new clothes? He was now implying the diamond jewels were also part of the uniform. If they had been alone in the car she would have argued the point with him, but they weren't. Frank was with them and he was listening.

Amy leant forward and gave Max a seductive, lingering kiss on his lips.

"Why, darling," she said, sarcasm was dripping heavily from her tongue. "I don't know how to thank you."

"Then I'll remind you later tonight my love *when we're alone.* You can show me properly just how thankful you are."

He was playing the newly married husband for all it was worth.

It was a brief ride, hardly worth getting the car out of the garage, and all too soon the car came to a stop beside the chopper.

The chopper's blades were turning and inside the cockpit, the pilot was checking the instrument panel.

"Ready when you are Mr. Jordan."

Climbing on board, they all buckled securely into their seats and were given the all clear for take-off. In no time at all, they were airborne and speeding on their way to the company's headquarters in New York City.

Amy hadn't realised they would be landing in the city on the roof of Jordan Towers.

Jordan Towers was one of the skyscrapers of New York City and it housed Jordan Diamond Empire offices with its designer jewellery store at street level. Below ground was the guarded diamond vaults where the precious diamond stones were housed and secured. Situated on the upper levels were the general office units and all the legal departments which powered the global company.

The journey had been done in such a rush, Amy felt as if she'd been travelling non-stop at high speed since leaving Waterfront.

A security guard had been radioed to meet them on arrival, and when they landed on the roof Amy, Max and Frank were escorted into the elevator and down to the main entrance of the building.

Going outside into the cool air of the night, they found a limousine waiting to take them to the restaurant.

Traffic was whizzing past and yellow cabs were scouring and prowling the New York streets searching for passengers. Amy's eardrums were bombarded and blasted with the noise and sounds of the city. Tall skyscrapers lined the horizon and multi-storey buildings flanked the sidewalks. The trendy storefronts with their glass wall panels and window displays were shimmering and glimmering in the evening sunset.

The sidewalks were lit and the city was alive and buzzing...and she was part of it.

Entering the restaurant they were welcomed by the maître d' of the *River Boat Café*. Then, walking through the dining room doors, they discovered a room full of people. A loud resounded cry followed by stupendous clapping and cheering came from the friends and colleagues who had gathered there.

'Surrrppprise...Congratulations'

Frank had booked the whole boat for an impromptu reception to celebrate the wedding. Sat at the wedding party's table with two vacant places in the middle were Alexander and Kim Jordan.

"I'll get you back for this," Max said to Frank. Then he whispered something in Frank's ear and Frank disappeared from the room.

Amy didn't know where to look first.

There were so many people in the room and she was feeling overwhelmed by all the attention she was receiving. Panic was beginning to set in and she grabbed the sleeve of Max's dinner jacket for moral support. Clutching at his arm she was desperately seeking reassurance.

Amy was usually the one in control.

When she was with James in the law office she'd always been able to take care of herself. Tonight was different. Tonight she was out of her depth.

The women were all wearing gems and diamonds and the room was sparkling and glimmering like a Christmas tree. The men were dressed to the nines in dinner suits and Italian handmade shoes. Everywhere Amy looked, she was confronted by wealth and money.

The people here were mostly Max's friends or they were connected in some way to the family business. She knew no one...except for Frank and Max's parents.

Sensing Amy's angst and guessing she was scared stiff, Max placed a reassuring arm around her waist and started guiding her through the crowd. He began to introduce her to everyone and gradually he was getting her to relax.

About an hour into the evening they had nearly reached their seats at the top table when a stunning blond, accompanied by an equally handsome man, approached Max. Amy thought the woman was one of the most beautiful women she had ever seen. Her hair was the colour of golden corn and it was piled high on her head and designed to cascade, falling softly to frame her face.

"Max darling...so you've come back to us," said the woman. "Now that you're here, you can play Sir Galahad and rescue me from boredom." She placed a possessive hand on his arm and planted a voluptuous kiss on Max's lips. A vivid smudge of scarlet lipstick was showing on Max's lips and without ceremony, the woman began intimately rubbing the red smear away with her long, slender, manicured fingertips.

Max pulled his head back from the reaching hands, found a handkerchief in his pocket and began wiping the remains of the lipstick from his face.

"Yes, I'm back," he said without excitement. Mild boredom was in his tone. "Someone has to keep an eye on the shop and I wouldn't want to rely on you to keep us *afloat*...now would I?"

Amy wasn't sure about the meaning behind his words but she could see the others had got his hidden message.

"Whatever do you mean Max? I always have the company's best interest at heart and I wouldn't let *our business* go under. Besides if I did, Clive would save us, wouldn't you darling?" She was matching Max's tone.

The woman's tinkling laugh grated on Amy's sensitive ears. And the man at the woman's side had raised his brows sceptically.

"Amy," said Max. "This is Stephanie who I'm sure you've heard me mention before now. And this is her brother, Clive Stone. Stephanie *was* my brother's wife"

The penny dropped.

Amy suddenly realised why Max was on edge and why he was almost aggressive. Stephanie had been Brad's wife and Max was tense because the woman was a threat to his diamond company.

When Brad had died, this woman, Stephanie, had received Brad's shares in the company. And if she got her hands on another two per cent of Jordan stock she would gain the controlling majority and Jordan Diamond Empire and Max would be out of business.

Nothing and no one would be able to stop Stephanie from selling or merging Jordan Diamonds with another firm. And the firm she would choose would be Stones.

Max could still lose the upper hand when it came to who had the majority shares in the company, but that wasn't going to happen now, because he had married to eliminate that possibility.

The only thing that could possibly jeopardise the Jordan Empire would be if someone exposed and proved their marriage to be a fake.

Clive Stone stepped forward and shook hands with Amy.

"Now I can see why Max has kept you a secret from us." Clive gave Amy a friendly smile. "May I be one of the first people to welcome you to America?"

"Thank you," she said returning Clive's polite smile.

"How are you enjoying America so far?" he asked.

She felt a sudden tug as Max tightened his hold and pulled her close.

"It's been wonderful," she said. "We've only been here since this morning and so far we haven't really had the opportunity to explore the city. But I've noticed that everything in New York seems to be on such a huge scale compared to England. The buildings are so tall and large."

"You'll get used to them if you stay here a while," Clive said.

"And why wouldn't she be staying?" Max asked forcefully.

He was on the defensive which was unusual for Max. He was usually the one who was the aggressor in any given situation.

Clive looked slightly taken aback at the question but shrugged his shoulders in response.

"I only meant that if Amy was to spend any time in the city she would soon grow accustomed to life here...compared to life in the Hamptons," he explained.

"Aha..." was all Max was prepared to say.

"I'm sure I'll be spending quite a lot of my time in the city," Amy said trying to ease the tension between the two men. "We're working on a lawsuit and I'm sure Max will set me to work in the office almost immediately. He used to have me research for him. He's always been a hard taskmaster."

"I don't think you'll be starting work in the near future, my love," Max said. Then he looked over at Clive. "You see, we have a son who needs his mother's attention."

"But surely not as much as you need me, my darling," Amy pouted at Max.

She then gave Max a teasing pat on his cheek with her fingers.

"Max might not want me to work for him, but I can assure you I'll be at the office in next to no time," she said playfully.

Clive laughed. "It seems not only have you got a beautiful wife Max; you've also got a willing slave."

"You've got that wrong, Clive. And allow me to say that I stand corrected. It's the other way around. I'm the one who's the slave in this relationship. I'm also the one who has to do what I'm told. Isn't that right my love? So, it seems that my wife will be helping me with Jordan Diamonds whenever she pleases and whenever she likes."

Max planted a kiss on her lips whilst he held her clamped vigorously and lovingly to his side.

She didn't know what he was playing at but she'd gathered he was putting on a show of devotion not only for the two people standing in front of them but for the whole room.

Stephanie looked like she could spit daggers at Max, and Amy was wondering why.

"If you don't mind, we have to move on," Max said calmly. "We have other guests we haven't yet seen or spoken to and I can also see my parents waiting for us to join them. If you'll excuse us."

Leaving a puzzled Clive and an enraged Stephanie staring after them, Max steered Amy away. He pulled her along behind him as they made their way towards the top table.

It took them nearly an hour to reach the top table and at that moment Frank returned, and he wasn't alone. He was accompanied by Hanna and he was carrying a sleepy bundle. Amy went to meet them and she whispered her thanks to Frank.

Max had sent Frank to collect Jake knowing that the evening wouldn't be complete for Amy if she didn't share it with their son.

When everyone was present and seated, the welcome speeches began. Alexander Jordan, sensing that the moment was right, struggled to his feet. The stroke had affected some of his abilities but he was able to stand. He tested the microphone before he started the ball rolling by welcoming Amy and Jake into the family.

When it came time for Max to respond and say something to his guests, there was a subtle change to the atmosphere in the room. All eyes and attention had zoomed in and were now focused on Max. Everyone was silently waiting to hear what he was about to say.

At that moment Amy realised exactly how much power and authority Max commanded over the people before him. The room was quiet. You could have heard a pin drop.

No one could deny the man oozed strength and energy and, as much as she disliked him for what he was making her do, she had to admit he could still affect her. Not only could he affect her physically but he could also cause a reaction emotionally.

She knew she had to keep her head screwed on if she was to survive.

Listening to him speak she couldn't help but feel a sense of pride that this man was her husband.

After Max had spoken, everyone present in the room had been made aware in no uncertain terms, that Amy and Jake were now considered fully-fledged Jordans. He was sending out a message. He was laying down the law and it was like a warning.

Amy and Jake belonged to the Jordans. No one was to harm or mess with them.

But at the same time, Max was also sending out a subtle message to Amy. He was telling her she belonged to him. She was now part of a prominent and important family in the community. She was being forewarned that she had to step up to the mark and behave accordingly.

With her new marital status came new responsibilities and at that moment it brought home to her just how alone she was. She felt she had no one to turn to for support or guidance. She was totally on her own and then she remembered she wasn't completely alone...she had Jake. She would always have Jake.

But her sweet dream was short lived as she remembered Max had the power to take Jake away from her anytime he wished.

"We'd better start the dancing," he whispered quietly in her ear and he picked the sleepy Jake up from her lap and handed his son over to Kim Jordan.

"Jake, you stay with Grandma and sit and watch your mother dance. We'll be back soon. Promise," he said lovingly but firmly to his son.

Amy had no opportunity to protest as Max pulled her onto a small dance floor.

"We have to make this look real," he told her. "They've all come here to see my new bride and we're not going to disappoint them."

"What do you mean?" she said.

He pulled her into his arms.

"Come on...let's dance. That's why they're here. They've come to see the newlyweds together so let's give them the show they've been waiting for."

Max held Amy in his arms and she was pressed so close to his body that they were seen to be as one.

He kissed her long, hard and passionately for all to see. He kissed her until she was gasping for air and then gradually, involuntarily, something happened to her. Something she had no control over. She began to return the loving passion of his kiss.

From the crowd of well-wishers came the sound of magnificent applause and as she heard shouts of approval ringing in her ears, she felt Max whisk her off her feet to the throbbing beat of the music.

Their evening had only just begun.

Chapter 7

It wasn't until the early hours of the morning that Max and Amy were able to leave the restaurant boat in the city. The party was still in full swing, and when they disembarked onto the quayside Max had stood shaking hands with Frank, thanking him for organising the party and promising they would all see one another soon.

"Frank...thank you so much," Amy reached up and kissing Frank on the cheek. "It's been an evening that we won't forget."

"I'll get the photos to you as soon as they're developed," he said.

"Just wait until it's your turn," Max said. "I'll get you back."

They all laughed. And having said farewell, by the time Max and Amy reached the roof heliport at Jordan Towers, landed in the Hamptons and then drove on to Waterfront, Amy was exhausted. She didn't dare think how Max must be feeling.

They found the place in darkness.

Walking around the car to the passenger's side, Max held the door whilst Amy climbed tiredly out of the vehicle.

"Do you think we ought to check on Jake and see if he's alright?" she asked.

A few hours earlier, before the party had ended, Kim and Alexander had taken Jake and Hanna home with them. Jake and Hanna were sleeping over at the beach house.

Someone at the wedding dinner had jokingly made a remark that Amy and Max ought to have at least one romantic honeymoon night alone in their own home, and everyone had laughingly agreed. It had been assumed that it was what the two newlyweds would want.

Forced into an awkward position and under duress, Amy had given in. Reluctantly she'd agreed to the suggestion...on one condition. If Jake needed her at any time during the night, someone was to phone Waterfront. She would walk the short distance to the beach house and could be there in a flash.

"It's gone two o'clock," Max told her. "I expect everyone at the beach house has gone to bed."

Amy looked at her watch to see the time but the night was too dark. Max had mentioned two o'clock and he was probably right. Everyone would almost certainly be in bed by now.

"Come inside it's chilly out here" He shifted the cashmere wrap on her shoulders to protect her from the cold.

Together they went up the steps and opening the front door, Max walked passed her into the large, darkened entrance hallway. He switched on a table lamp. Except for the lights outside on the veranda, the house was in shadows.

Closing the heavy, oak-framed door, Max shut out the outside world and made his way towards the study.

Leaving her wrap and handbag on the hall table Amy followed and the sound of her heels could be heard echoing on the stark, black and white tiles of the hallway. The house sounded hollow and silent. No one was home.

Entering the study, Max reached out and flicked on one of the wall switches. Expecting the room to be instantly flooded with light, Amy was surprised when only a few spot-lights cast soft, dark, shadows across the walls. Going over to a nearby table lamp she was about to press the switch when he called out to stop her.

"No don't. Leave it. Come here and sit down. We have to talk," he said.

The evening fire in the hearth had died down to glowing embers and Max threw on a couple of logs, poking it back into life. Soon the room was filled with a warm glow.

Heading over to the drinks table he lifted the stopper from the neck of a heavy, crystal decanter, poured himself a large whisky and downed it in one. Looking at Amy he waved the decanter gesturing to her.

She shook her head declining his silent offer. She'd had enough to drink this evening and all she wanted was her bed - or rather *his* bed - but seeing he was about to pour another whisky for himself she changed her mind.

"Oh alright," she said with reluctance. "I'll join you if I must. I'll have a brandy if that okay. I wouldn't want you to drink alone."

"What a considerate wife I have."

"What's so urgent that we have to talk now?" she asked him.

"Things," he said. "We have to talk about how things are. And about how things are going to be between us."

She couldn't face what was coming and she didn't want to listen to what he had to say.

Amy reached up and unclasped the expensive diamond necklace from around her neck and held it out to him along with the other jewels.

For some unknown reason, she kept his wedding band on her finger.

"What's this for?" he asked looking at the million dollar collection of diamonds in his hand. "I gave them to you. They're yours to keep."

"Max I've changed my mind," she said. "I don't think I can go through with this pretence. I can't pretend to the world that we're happily married. Someone is bound to realise sooner or later that we don't have a real marriage. If we have to talk about anything we have to talk about us and how to get out of this marriage."

She had told him what she was thinking and she waited worriedly for his reaction.

"What's brought this on?" he asked, tossing the jewels thoughtlessly, regardless of their worth, down among the crystal decanters and drinking glasses.

"I don't like deceiving people. And having talked with your mother this evening I particularly don't want to hurt your parents," she said sincerely.

"They won't be hurt. Not if you keep your end of the bargain," Max said.

"Max, we won't be able to fool them. They'll see us practically every day and they'll soon realise something's wrong. They're not stupid."

"Amy, this marriage isn't about them, it's about us."

No, it's not, she thought. *This marriage is about the Jordan Diamond Empire and Stephanie.*

Amy was silenced and a hush fell, broken only by the crackling sound of burning wood on the fire.

She went to the sofa and sat down. She soon realised she'd made a wrong choice of where to sit when Max brought their drinks over and joined her.

She could smell the provocative scent of his cologne and it was making her senses whirl.

Max had already taken off his jacket and loosened his tie. Leaning back into the corner of the sofa he looked very much at ease and relaxed.

"Did you enjoy the party and our wedding this morning?" he asked changing the topic of conversation slightly.

He swirled his drink around in his glass. She wondered where he was going with this conversation.

"Um...and there was quite a crowd there this evening?" she answered.

She was aware of his nearness and the side of his muscular leg as it pressed heavily against hers.

He seemed immersed, mesmerised by the contents of his glass, and he was deep in thought.

"And the wedding? Our wedding?" he asked.

"What about the wedding?"

"Nothing...I just wondered. Was it what you expected your wedding to be like?"

She didn't reply immediately. She didn't really know how to answer that question. It had been her wedding day and she'd always imagined she would have planned or at least had some input in what was to have happened on that day. But things had been taken out of her hands.

Max had taken over and she felt the only contributing factor she'd had to play in the whole event was saying the words...*I do*.

"Why did you want James to give me away?" she asked.

"James?"

It was as if he'd been jerked back into the moment by the mention of James.

"I saw you talking to James before the wedding," he said taking a hefty swig of his drink.

"Yes...we were talking."

"I didn't like it."

"But we were only talking."

"I still didn't like it. He was holding you."

"No, he wasn't. I was tense and on edge. I was about to get married and I was terrified. James was only massaging my neck," she told him trying to reassure him.

She wondered why Max was so obsessed with her interactions with James.

Max took the brandy glass from her hand and placed it together with his whisky tumbler on the coffee table beside the sofa.

Then he reached for her.

"Was it like this? Does James touch you here...and here?" He was angry, but his hands were saying something different. They were softly cupping her face and his fingers tangled and teased, splayed and opened, moving gently into her hair.

His hold on her was tender, almost worshipful.

"No Max," she pleaded and wondered what was coming next. She wasn't prepared for this. She needed to keep her distance. She wouldn't let herself surrender to his touch but he was awakening emotions inside her that she'd long forgotten.

"Yes..." he moaned against her lips.

Then the weight of him was pressing her back against the sofa and he was kissing her hard and with a cruel purpose. There was passion in his touch and he was demanding a response which she knew she shouldn't give.

"No...don't...stop Max. Let me go."

He was looking deeply into her dark anxious eyes and as if he realized what he was doing, his hold on her slackened. His touch changed. It became softer.

Amy's gaze was transfixed on his granite etched face.

"I know you want me," he told her unfeelingly. "And I know I can make you want me as much as I want you."

Then she felt the familiar touch of his fingers as he began to caress her. His pace had slowed and he was teasingly tracing the high neckline of her gown.

He was moving tantalisingly to the plunging back of her designer dress where a bare expanse of skin had been left exposed. He was caressing and stroking her and she was instantly aroused.

Slowly his hands began their familiar tender rhythm. He was gently kneading her flesh and sliding his long, strong fingers between the silk of her dress to fondle and caress her bare skin.

His mouth came down hard on hers and he forced her lips to part and open.

Involuntarily she lifted her arms running her hands through his hair. She was matching his urgency to hers and she felt a deep shudder go through him at her touch.

She'd waited so long for this moment. And now she was responding to his touch as she always had...fully...totally and without restraint. She'd no thoughts of fighting or resisting him. In an instant, Max had aroused her fully.

His fingers played with the fastening of her dress, pulling, tugging downwards until finally the tight pressure on her breast was released only to be replaced with the pressure of his hands.

"Max," she gasped, shocked at the erotic sensual touch of his hands against her nipples.

He shifted, breaking free for a moment, pulling her with him off of the sofa. Her dress fell away from her leaving her breasts bare and except for her lace panties, she was naked. And then Max was drawing her down to the large scatter cushions he'd quickly thrown on the floor. Together they lay on the soft sheepskin rug side by side in the warming heat from the fire.

Max began caressing her arms moving unhurriedly towards her taut breasts.

His soft, silk shirt was rubbing against her skin and slowly she began to undo the buttons, exposing the fine hairs on his chest. With each button she released, she kissed him lingeringly on his lips.

"Don't stop." he groaned.

She didn't.

With his tie and shirt removed they lay skin on skin. Their bodies were pressed together and the heat between them was beginning to build.

She'd an all-consuming urgent need to join as one with him.

Max rolled onto his back pulling her on top of him. Their passion was moving too quickly. She wanted to savour the moment and take him with her to the uncontrollable heights and peaks of their desire.

Resting her head against the warmth of his broad chest Amy listened to the heavy beating of his pounding heart. She knew he was excited...and she knew she excited him. She could feel the hardness of him grinding and pressing beneath his trousers against her limbs.

Slowly she began to struggle with the heavy buckle of his belt and as she did so she leant forward, kissing him, penetrating him with her mouth and with her tongue.

Her breasts rubbed against his chest. Her nipples were taut and throbbing. Desperately she wanted his touch.

Amy felt for the fastening of his trousers and fumbling with the zipper she released his throbbing rod from its confines.

Max reached for her. Taking her rounded breasts in his hands he pulled her to him until he was able to run his tongue across their rigid peaks. She was in agonising ecstasy and she didn't want him to stop what he was doing. With his hands on her hips, he pressed her hard against his manhood exciting them both further for what was to come.

But nothing came. It didn't happen. At that moment the deafening shrill of the telephone could be heard on the study desk.

They both froze.

"No. Not now." he moaned and held her tightly. He was crushing her to him as if he would never let her go.

The noise of the phone stopped as suddenly as it had started.

"Wrong number…"

Max rolled himself over and taking her with him, he pushed her deeper, sinking her further into the softness of the cushions beneath them with his weight.

Once more he cupped the fullness of her breasts to his mouth and she held his head as he hungrily sought and devoured her. She was unable to hold on any longer and she released a long, stifling groan of pleasure as his hands tugged at her lace panties. His fingers slipped inside finding the soft folds and crevice of her womanhood. He had found the spot he sought. Uncontrollably she squirmed and bucked frantically beneath him as he pressed and rubbed frenziedly with his fingers against her clitoris.

She was wet and ready for him and she trembled and pushed wildly towards him as he touched and probed.

The phone rang again and with an effort, he was able to drag himself from her. Resting on one elbow he looked down at her.

Her nipples were hard, swollen and bruised. She looked dishevelled and wanton and he liked what he saw. Max leant towards her and whispered in her ear.

"I have to answer. No one in their right mind would call here at this time of night. It could be the Beach House...they could be calling about Jake."

He was right. He had to answer.

As he pulled away from her, a cool draught of cold air rushed between them. The moment of passion had been broken.

Max stood and walked to the desk. He lifted the receiver running a hand in frustration through his dark hair as he answered.

"Max Jordan here..."

The call could be about Jake. He could be in trouble.

The minute Max had lifted the receiver she knew their moment of lovemaking and passion had ended. The mood had been broken. And there would be no going back to their intimate moment beside the fire. The inferno burning within her had been doused.

Amy began pulling on her dress, frantically covering her exposed breasts and body. And as she was dressing, she heard Max speaking on the phone and what she heard shook her to the core.

"No Stephanie. Not now. It's not convenient and nothing's so urgent that it can't wait until morning."

The voice on the other end of the phone said something.

"Yes, of course, Amy's here. And my wife being here has nothing to do with..."

Stephanie must have said something to annoy Max because the next thing Amy heard was, "If Jordan Empire collapses overnight then so be it. Goodnight Stephanie. I'll see you in the office tomorrow."

Amy was remembering Stephanie and the way the men had clustered about her at the restaurant. Was Max one of her many admirers? Had he been one of her many lovers in the months before his brother's death?

Amy hated the sudden horrid direction her thoughts were taking her. It was nothing to do with her who Max had been involved with. If he'd been involved with Stephanie...well...it was none of her business.

He had been a free agent and he could have kept a harem for all she cared. The only thing that worried her was that the affair would have been with his brother's wife.

Amy was struggling to do up the zipper when Max came to stand in front of her.

"What are you doing?" he asked.

She could feel her cheeks burning from embracement and mortification at what she'd very nearly done...what *they* had nearly done.

They were a couple and they were married but what a fool she'd been to believe she could possibly mean anything to Max. She was a moment's fancy. She was conveniently here and Max - being a man with sexual needs and urges - had used her as if she was something he owned.

"Max...I can't stay here. I have to leave. This marriage will never work and it will never fool anyone...especially Stephanie." There was desperation in her voice.

Amy was still trembling with longing. She knew that if he kissed her or even touched her, she would fall willingly back into his arms there and then. She wouldn't be able to help herself. But she couldn't let herself want him. And it was only the thought of Stephanie that kept her from giving in to her physical needs and desires.

Max had moved towards the door. Opening it, he left the study and strode to the staircase, leaving Amy to follow if she wished.

"There's no point arguing and I'm not staying to listen to this," he said over his shoulder.

She trailed behind him to the bottom of the stairs.

"I'm going to bed," he told her.

"We need to talk about this," she called after him.

"But not at this time of night. Why is it women always want to talk business when it's least convenient?"

* * * *

Max reached the top of the staircase and disappeared into their bedroom. Left to collect the evidence of their discarded, scattered clothing, Amy switched off the lights and followed. Reluctantly she climbed the stairs behind him.

She found him in their bedroom undressing.

Still half naked, Max was removing his trousers as he made his way to the en-suite.

"I'm not going to bed with you Max," she called after him.

He didn't reply.

The door to the en-suite had been left open and she could hear the sound of the shower running. She waited until he emerged damp and moist from the steam filled room. He was wearing nothing beneath his robe.

"Did you hear what I said?" she asked. "I said I'm not going to go to bed with you."

"I heard you the first time."

"Well?"

"We're going to have to share our bed sometime," he told her. "And we might as well start now."

"But you said we would only need to pretend our marriage is real in front of others. Why do I have to sleep with you tonight? There's no one here in the house to see if we share the same bed. Surely there's no need for pretence if no one's here," she argued.

"My employees are loyal to me, but news always leaks out. The world would soon know if we weren't sleeping in the same bed."

"But I can't. It doesn't seem right."

"And then there's Jake..." he said.

"What about Jake?"

She thought Max was once again going to threaten to take Jake from her.

"It's best if Jake sees us together. He might be innocently playing with one of his new friends and let slip that we have separate beds. The illusion of a happy, perfect marriage would then be shattered."

"We'll be living a lie," she warned.

"Then if it's a lie we'll be living...get used to it," he told her harshly.

Max could lose the company to Stephanie if the authenticity and reality of their marriage were proven to be false. He had a lot to lose. He couldn't afford to take the chance that someone would discover their secret. Their marriage had to seem real to everyone at all times and it seemed he was prepared to tread carefully for the sake of his family and the company.

"Come to bed Amy. We've had a long day and we have an even longer one tomorrow," he said trying to persuade her.

"Why? What's happening tomorrow?" she asked.

"We're talking Jake to school and introducing him to his class and then we're heading into the city. I still have the Diablo case to finish even if I am on my honeymoon," he told her.

Max pulled back the bed covers and at the same time, he loosened the sash of his robe.

"You're not going to bed like that..." she said stunned at what Max was intending to do.

He was stark naked and he was about to climb into bed...their bed.

"Like what?" he asked.

"I can't sleep with you dressed like that. You're not wearing anything. You're naked."

She could smell the tangy scent of his aftershave and it was teasing her nostrils. He had shaved when he was in the shower and he never shaved at night unless...

They had almost made love downstairs in front of the fire and here she was fantasising and imagining that he intended to continue where they had left off. She daren't think or let her thoughts wander any further. Max had only ever shaved at night when he'd intended to make love to her. She'd once complained that his stubble was scratching and hurting her and he'd promised to always shave for her.

"Amy I've always slept naked...correction...*we've* always slept naked. So what's the problem now? There's nothing here that you haven't seen before." He yawned.

Climbing into bed, he pulled the covers over him and reached out to switch the bedside lamp off on his side of the bed, leaving hers on. He lay there relaxed, waiting for her to come to bed.

Going into their en-suite, she removed her make-up before going to the dressing room to look for a nightgown to wear to bed. Not daring to put the bright overhead light on in the dressing room in case it disturbed Max, she rummaged in the cupboards using the light that fell through the open door from the bedroom.

There were nightgowns - lots of them - and they were all sheer, silk and sexy, and she wasn't wearing any of them. There was no way she was climbing into bed with only a see-through slip to protect her from Max's prying eyes.

Digging deep, she delved into a T-shirt drawer and hunted out one of her old T-shirts. At home in England, there had been no need for her to look sexy when she went to bed and she usually wore a long, baggie T-shirt. The only man in her life was Jake and with his tiny, sticky fingers there would have been no point wearing something sophisticated or feminine. A T-shirt was what she usually wore and it would have to do for Max.

Going back into the bedroom she found Max sitting up in bed with his arms folded behind his head resting back against the pillows. The bedside lamp on her side of the bed was still alight and it was casting dark shadows around the room and across his bare chest.

His torso was tanned, strong and muscular.

He looked fit and healthy and she couldn't help the way her stomach somersaulted and her heart raced at the sight of him. He'd always had that effect on her. She had only to see him...to want him.

Max was looking at her and his eyes were coolly assessing. They travelled up and down the length of her body and Amy shivered involuntarily at the intensity of his stare.

"Go and change," he told her coolly. "Take it off. There are plenty of things for you to wear without you having to wear that."

"What's wrong with this?" She was nervously pulling at the T-shirt as she was climbing into bed.

"Everything. Now go and change," he ordered.

"I don't see the point of—"

"I won't tell you a third time."

"But..."

She didn't have the chance to finish what she was about to say.

Before she realised what Max intended to do he reached over from his side of the bed, took hold of her shirt and ripped it from her shoulders. There had been no warning. He simply tore the shirt open revealing the soft, slender curves of her body and the round, heavy fullness of her breasts beneath.

Amy gasped in horror.

Clutching the remainder of the T-shirt in her shaking hands, she frantically pulled the torn pieces together, covering her body.

"Change," was all he said.

Amy went back to the dressing room and found one of the silk nightgowns she'd rejected earlier. She had pushed it to the back of the drawer. Quickly she took off the shredded pieces of material and put on the night slip.

The silk gown clung to her body revealing all.

She was trembling. Not from excitement but from fear at what was to happen.

Slowly she walked back to the bedroom and stood waiting in the doorway. She was about to cross a threshold into the unknown.

"Come to bed," he urged. He patted her side of the bed invitingly.

"I can't," she told him.

She was unwilling to take a step further.

"Then I'll have to come and get you," he threatened.

He didn't have to.

Reluctantly she went to her side of the bed and slipped carefully beneath the satin sheets.

Max reached over to switch off the light on her side of the bed and in doing so accidentally brushed her breasts with his arm. She froze waiting for his next move but nothing happened. He only pulled her into him, spooning her against his body, gently cradling her in his arms.

The room had been plunged into total darkness. She was alone with Max as she'd never been before. No one was within hearing distance and there were no neighbours to hear her should she scream. Only the silence of the world was around them.

"Go to sleep," he said. "We'll talk in the morning."

But as tired as she was she couldn't sleep.

It had been years since she'd been this close to him but it seemed like only yesterday. And as she lay there in the darkness wrapped in his arms listening to the sound and the feel of his steady breathing against her neck, she also heard the pounding of her excited anxious heart.

She knew she was where she belonged...she had come home...she had come home to Max.

* * * *

Something, a noise or a sound, had woken her out of her sleep. Reaching out she felt for the clock on the bedside table and as she peered at the face on the dial, she saw the time. It had gone four o'clock.

Beside her in bed, Max was restlessly tossing and turning. He must have woken her with his agitated movements. Something was worrying him because he was moving restively. He was thrashing about next to her beneath the covers.

Max was calling out Brad's name in his sleep and she knew he must be having some sort of bad dream about his twin. Amy wondered if seeing Stephanie at the restaurant had awakened bad memories.

The bedclothes were dishevelled. They had slipped down leaving his bronzed torso exposed and bare. Instinctively she pulled the covers back over him and in a soothing, comforting tone she tried to reassure him that all was well.

"Brad...stop, don't go," he called again.

"Go back to sleep," she told him quietly with concern in her voice.

Max stirred and began to wake fully.

"Amy?" he asked in a puzzled, almost disbelieving way. And then she saw the remembrance and relief return.

"Shh...go back to sleep," she told him.

He turned towards her lifting himself onto one elbow. Their eyes were locked and he held her captive. She was mesmerized, transfixed and she couldn't move away or break his stare.

Gently he reached out and ran his fingertips tenderly and caressingly along the side of her face. Max's hand moved provocatively towards her neck and he began to play teasingly with the shoulder straps of her silk nightgown.

"Max...." she whispered quietly. She was scared and at the same time excited by what she knew was about to happen.

"I thought I was dreaming," he said drowsily and he pulled her towards him, into the curve of his body.

He gave a low satisfying groan betraying his arousal.

As Amy lay next to him she couldn't pull away. He was holding her tightly against him and she knew it would be useless to struggle. Pressed firmly against his body she could feel him becoming erect and hard with desire. He was awakening a familiar response in her.

"You know it's no good, don't you?" he asked her.

"What's no good?"

"Us...it's no good. We can't fight it."

"Fight what?"

He didn't have to say. She knew what he meant. There had always been an attraction between them. From the first time they had seen each other, they had struggled and lost the battle to resist their primal basic yearnings.

Max had always wanted her and she had always surrendered. He'd never been able to keep his hands off her and he couldn't keep his hands off her now.

"We can't fight this...and this..." he said planting kisses along her jawline.

Then slowly he began placing light soft kisses against the arched curve of her neck. And just as slowly, her hands moved rhythmically over his bare shoulders feeling his taut, strong, rippling muscles beneath her fingers.

In the darkness, all she could feel was the rough unyielding sensation of him pressing firmly and solidly against her. This man knew her body like no other. He knew what excited her and he knew how to adjust her needs to suit his. It had been years since he'd held her so close but she was no stranger to the feel of him.

Max had always been a considerate lover and she didn't doubt he would make sure she was pleasured and satisfied during their lovemaking. But when she heard the hunger in his voice and felt the rough brutal touch of his hands as he began urgently exploring her body she became frightened, yet excited at the same time.

"No Max...don't. Stop," she mumbled weakly and breathlessly into his chest while making a last effort to resist this strong, sexy man who was her husband.

But she couldn't hold back and she wasn't going to hold back. She ached with longing.

"I can't," he said hoarsely. "I can't stop. Don't make me."

She heard the rip and tear of material as Max hastily struggled to remove the delicate silk night slip she was wearing. The torn shreds were thrown from her body into a distant corner of the room and his hands reached for her exposed breasts.

At his touch, her nipples became instantly erect. Her back arched offering them to him and his mouth sought and found her. He sucked delicately on the tender, swollen peaks until they became inflamed, pulsating buds.

Stirring somewhere deep within, she felt the familiar hot, fiery craving awakening inside. He was arousing her body to desires and longings she'd forgotten she had.

With the heaviness of his body lying against hers and the urgent pressure of his hands as he began to freely explore, Amy trembled and whimpered hopelessly with need. They were pressed naked body to naked body and nothing could separate them.

She could feel the rough throbbing hardness of his manhood rubbing and grinding against her and when she started moving against him she knew she was exciting him.

Teasingly she ran her fingers through the dusty scattering of hairs on his chest before daring to travel further down the length of his body. She boldly moved to the sensitive areas of his loins and slowly, she lightly raked her nails along the length of his powerful, muscular inner thighs.

A crippling, uncontrollable spasm rippled through his body at her playful touch, causing him to trust violently towards her with abandoned urgency. He shuddered as if he was unable to bear her teasing any longer.

Rolling her over onto her back, Max positioned himself above her. He pressed her deeper and deeper into the soft, fluffy pillows beneath them.

Thrusting one of his legs between hers, he forced her thighs apart. He held her spreadeagled and open. She was vulnerable, exposed helpless to the desires and demands he was making.

Reaching down with one hand he felt for the fine, silky hairs of her womanly triangle. Seeking further, his fingers found and caressed the sticky wetness of her inner folds. She was moist and ready for him and she was trembling with uncontrollable anticipation as he drew nearer and nearer to the place he was seeking.

Then he found what he'd been searching for. His fingers were parting her soft, wet folds.

Delving deeper he slid a finger inside her and withdrew, only to enter her again but this time he filled her with two fingers. Carefully Max began stretching her. He was preparing her for what was to come.

Max was rubbing and caressing her sensitive spot vigorously and it was an agonising delight for her. But when he started rolling her hard clitoris between his thumb and forefinger it was unbearable, ecstatic torture.

Involuntarily her hips arched. She couldn't hold back a long indrawn gasp of shocked and delirious surprise as red hot spasms of pure pleasure surge through her body.

Their bodies were damp and moist from desire. Their hot energy was becoming frenzied and she was on the brink of release.

Desperately she strained towards him and with heated urgency, she spread her legs opening fully. Raising her hip off the bed she was ready for him.

Max tested her entrance then plunged hard and smoothly deep inside.

Lifting her legs she curled them, clamping them behind him. She was forcing him down deeper and deeper into her and she held him clenched in a vice-like grip as he sank into the hilt.

He filled her.

As her inner muscles pressed around his stiff rod she held him fast. She wasn't letting go. For a brief moment, they both paused. They were fused together.

"Are you alright?" he asked.

He was inside her and she could feel his thick shaft jerk and buck against the walls of her sex.

"Um...yes."

"You sure?"

It was pointless for him to ask her if she was alright. He wouldn't have stopped if she'd asked him to and she wasn't asking...she couldn't. They had reached and gone past the point of no return.

Slowly she ran her hands down the length of his back until she reached his hips.

Teasingly she thrust her pelvis invitingly up at him and it was all he needed as a sign for him to continue.

Briefly, he kissed her, crushing her lips hard against her teeth and eagerly she returned the violent embrace before she buried her head shyly against his shoulder.

Max captured her hands in his and raised them above her head.

She wasn't protesting. She was surrendering utterly to his needs.

Her arms and legs were spreadeagled across the bed and she was at his mercy.

Then he began his beating rhythm of entering and withdrawing. He would enter and withdraw almost to the point of leaving her before entering her once again with hard downward pounding thrusts. Her juices were flowing as he glided in and out.

He had her bucking and slithering uncontrollably beneath him. Then he changed his pattern and pace. Instead of pounding down deep into her, he was thrusting upwards, rasping and grating hurriedly and harshly against her sensitive flesh. She was reaching the height of orgasm.

She lost control. Against her will, she was responding to his every thrust and she was coming and coming. Together he was riding the wave of orgasm with her.

Exhausted and spent from their crippling orgasms they lay entangled, gasping for air among the dishevelled satin bedclothes.

Max lay sprawled heavily over her. His weight was pinning her to the bed and she couldn't move. There was no escape as his body held her captive.

"Well, Mrs. Jordan...and how was your wedding night?" he moaned softly into her ear.

He rolled from her onto his back and a cool blast of air hit her skin as she lay exposed and naked beside him.

Her wedding night.

The surreal reality of her situation was beginning to surface. Their moment of passion had been and gone. Their appetite for one another had been appeased and sated and she was facing reality. Bruised and drained from the battering she had just endured, she turned onto her side looking away from him.

Max leant over reaching for her and he pulled her back into the curve of his body until she was beside him. They lay close, entwined and spooning.

"Amy?"

He was waiting for her to say something.

Grasping the bedclothes, he pulled them up, wrapping the bedding snuggly around them both. They lay there beneath the eiderdown cocooned in warmth.

"This isn't real Max. This isn't what our marriage is supposed to be like," she said.

"No? Then tell me how our marriage is supposed to be."

"It's only temporary. We're not supposed to get involved and, I don't want to get involved. I was out of your life and you were out of mine. And now I'm only here because you need to fool the world. I'm not denying we still have feelings for each other...but...they're only feelings of lust and desire. You only have to touch me and you can make me want you physically. You've proved that tonight. But I don't want you, Max. I don't want you emotionally. I don't want you with my heart," she told him.

She didn't tell him that she *couldn't let herself* want him.

Her head was telling her heart that she couldn't have him. And that meant she wouldn't let herself love him...not again.

Five years ago when they had parted she'd been badly hurt and nearly destroyed. She wasn't going to let it happen a second time. This time she wasn't going to let herself become emotionally involved. She had too much to lose.

"You can physically take me and make love to me Max...but you won't have me," she said.

"That's where you're wrong Amy. *I will have you.*"

"What do you mean?" she asked uncertainly.

"I've got six months to make you want me the way I want you and I can wait six months."

"But—"

"I'm not letting you go. Not this time. And our marriage is not temporary. Now go to sleep," he said.

Gently, he pulled her towards him, wrapping her in his strong arms. And with the dawn breaking on the horizon, she fell into a deep sleep encircled in the warmth of his protective embrace.

Chapter 8

Amy stirred from a heavy slumber and looking about her she discovered Max was nowhere to be seen. He'd obviously surfaced and gone downstairs to get on with his day, leaving her to have a much-deserved lay-in.

Stretching and yawning herself awake she felt aches and pains in her body that she hadn't felt in years. It felt good to be alive.

Swinging her legs over the side of the bed she walked into the en-suite and stood for a moment in front of the full-length mirror. She was examining the reflection of the person before her.

The woman looking back was tall, slim and radiant. She had an afterglow and luminosity of someone totally fulfilled. Passion and ardour had left their mark. Released was smouldering energy and brilliance which hadn't been there yesterday.

Amy felt wanted and desired...and it showed.

Yesterday evening Max had said something about taking Jake to school before going on to Jordan Towers in New York City and looking in the mirror she decided she would have to find something presentable to wear. Something that would cover up the slight bruising from his rough, but tender, handling during the night.

Thinking it best if she played it safe and dressed conservatively to meet Jake's teachers and the legal staff at Jordan Towers, she chose a skirt and blouse from the closet. Whilst she was there, she also found a matching jacket she could wear later. It was too warm for a coat.

Hurriedly she took a quick shower and dressed.

When ready, she went downstairs in search of Max and Jake and walked into the kitchen. Father and son sat at the breakfast bar, side by side. It looked like they had nearly finished their breakfast and Max was deep in thought reading the morning paper.

He looked up.

"Hello Mrs. Jordan," he said when he saw her standing in the doorway.

He was looking deep into her eyes.

"Hello, mummy."

"Morning, Jake."

Jake was rubbing his nose with the palm of his small hand absentmindedly. Rubbing his nose was one of the emotional reactions Jake had when he was excited about something.

"Come and see what I'm doing mummy. Daddy's letting me use his iPad and he's teaching me how to play a game," he said excitedly.

"Is he now? Are you sure it's alright for Jake to play with that?" she asked looking at Max and pointing to the iPad.

"He won't break it."

"No, I won't break it, mummy. I'm being very careful...see." And with his small fingers, he was painstakingly touching the screen moving the images about and learning new skills.

Amy walked around the breakfast bar to look at the iPad and as she did so Max stretched out an arm encircling her waist drawing her near.

Still sitting on the bar stool Max held her firmly pressed between his thighs. She couldn't escape.

Briefly, Jake looked questioning at the two adults. It was new for him to see his mother with a man in such a way, but he continued to play and concentrate on the iPad in front of him.

Lifting a hand Max captured her face and gave her a slow lingering kiss on her lips.

Remembering the long, passionate, intimate night they had just shared together she couldn't help but blush as she recalled their lovemaking.

"What can I get you?" he asked.

"Nothing thanks," and then she reached down and picked up his cup and took a sip of his hot, strong coffee.

"What...not even me?"

She gave him a suggestive smile.

"No. Not right now."

"Maybe later?"

"Umm...maybe."

Still held captive in Max's arms, she reached down and tweaked Jake on the chin. Running her fingers lovingly through her son's hair she straightened a stray lock that had fallen over his eyes.

He needs his hair cut again, she thought.

"And how's my best boy this morning? Did you have a good time with grandpa and grandma Jordan?"

"Yes I did," he told her. "But this morning grandma said I had to go home because I've got school today."

"That's right," said Max, "And that reminds me that we ought to be making a move. When your mother's ready we'll leave."

Amy reached for a spare piece of toast that was still on the breakfast counter and started nibbling.

"I'm ready," she told him as she wiped her buttery fingers on a table napkin. "What time are we supposed to be there?"

"We were supposed to be there at nine, but it doesn't matter. You were sleeping so I called the school to tell them we were running late. They'll see us when we get there."

Max had let her sleep on after their night together in bed. He'd probably thought she had needed a well-deserved rest.

"Jake is going to be playing with some new friends at school this afternoon; aren't you Jake? And Hanna is collecting him at three-thirty. Is that alright with you?"

To their surprise, Jake answered.

"I'll be alright," he told them in a grown-up way. "You said I have to be a big boy and learn lots of new things."

"That's right I did. And are you a big boy?" Max asked his young son.

"Yes, I am. And I promise I won't cry because you said mummy will be sad if I cry."

Amy bent down and gave Jake a kiss on the top of his head.

"You're not supposed to kiss me, mummy. I have to be a big boy. Only babies are allowed to have kisses," he said. He was rubbing his hair where she'd just kissed him.

"If we're ready...shall we go?" Max folded the newspaper he'd been reading during breakfast and pushed his empty coffee cup away.

"Yes," she said. "I'll be right with you. I'll just go and collect my jacket and bag from upstairs. I'll be with you in no time. Jake do you need to fetch your school books before we leave?"

"I'll go and fetch the car and I'll meet you two outside," Max told her.

Max gave Amy a brief, hard kiss on the lips. She found his onslaught beyond her power or ability to resist and returned his loving assault with similar intensity.

Having just innocently witnessed his parent's embrace Jake asked, "Are you a big baby daddy? Is that why mummy kisses you?"

Max threw back his head and let out a roar of laughter.

"I'll always be a big baby..." and Max kissed Amy again.

* * * *

After seeing Jake safely enrolled in school and leaving him with his teacher for the introduction day, Max and Amy returned to Waterfront and took the chopper into the city. The views over the city were amazingly impressive and from the sky, Jordan Towers looked like one of Max's diamonds.

The exterior walls of the building had floor to ceiling thick glass panels which reflected the intense heat in summer and retained the warmth in winter. Today its wall of glass was shining and shimmering in the strong sunlight and it sparkled like a jewel.

The building itself was high-spec.

Everything had been finished to perfection and the place was immaculate. There wasn't a speck of dust or dirt to be seen anywhere.

The floor space was open plan and most of the interior walls were glass partitioned. It gave the impression that there could be no secrets at Jordan Towers. Nothing could be hidden and everything was on view.

The moment they landed on the roof and entered the building, all hell broke loose. Everyone was clamouring to get to Max. He was being bombarded left, right and centre with questions and Amy had the feeling this was only the tip of the iceberg. There would be more to come.

Taking Amy along with him, and followed by an avalanche of personnel, Max went swiftly to the main office suite. When the outer doors leading to the office opened, another army of staff members was ready and waiting.

Apparently, there had been an uproar caused by Martin and Campbell. A document had been faxed through and a trial date had been set for next week. Panic and mayhem were in the air.

While Max was occupied talking business with a group of lawyers about developments, one of the junior associates came up to Amy and wished her all the best on her recent marriage.

"Hi...I'm Brenda. One of Max's many humble menial workers." There was a glint of humour in Brenda's eye which Amy liked. "I heard we missed a great reception on the boat last night. I'm afraid we were out of town yesterday. My husband's sister was having her first baby and we went to New Jersey to be with her. We were there to lend her moral support. Her husband's away in Iraq and we didn't want her fighting the birth battle on her own," she explained.

"Boy or a girl?" Amy asked.

"Eight pounds two ounces and she's a bouncing health girl," Brenda said excitedly.

"That's nice, but what a whopper. Your sister-in-law must be exhausted. Do you have any children of your own?"

"Not yet but we're hoping..."

Someone across the room was calling out and waving a hand in the air.

"Where's the Diablo report?"

"Here it is," Brenda shouted back.

Brenda was flipping through some files she was holding before handing over a document to one of the floor staff.

"Is it always like this?" Amy asked. She was curious to know if this was an average welcome for Max.

"Always...and I hate it. When Max first gets back from one of his trips there's always a backlog of work he has to get through. And there's always a queue to get to him," she explained.

At that moment the elevator doors opened and a woman walked into the room. A deathly hush fell over the office. It was Stephanie and, if it was possible, she was even more beautiful than Amy remembered from the previous evening.

There was an uneasy tension among the occupants of the room which Amy couldn't quite fathom. Everyone was looking from Max to Stephanie and then back to Max. The office was silent.

It was as if everyone was on a stage and the audience was waiting for the play to begin.

Stephanie made her move. Spotting Max sat at a desk, she walked over towards the group of men.

"Hello, Max." Her voice was silky, smooth and sensual.

Amy felt her stomach turning with a feeling of trepidation and apprehension.

"Hello, Stephanie," he replied. His voice had a scathing drawl to it.

There were over thirty-thousand people employed at Jordan Towers in New York City alone, not to mention his many other business sites around the globe; but it wasn't one of his managerial directors that wanted to be first in line for his attention...it was Stephanie.

"Max that lawsuit of ours, I'd really like you to come to my office and take a look at the paperwork. You need to make an assessment of the situation for yourself," Stephanie said.

"You phoned yesterday evening and I told you it's nothing urgent. I've seen the brief this morning and I've made an evaluation and sent you a recommendation. Business Law isn't my field of expertise Stephanie," he said with some degree of self-control. However, there was a slight tone of exasperation in his voice which Amy could hear. Max was obviously fast running out of patience and forbearance with Stephanie.

"I really would like you to have another look."

Amy knew Max was treading on eggshells where Stephanie was concerned. According to what he's told her, he daren't make an enemy of her. At least not yet. Not until he gained some extra company shares and they were securely in his name.

"If you will excuse me," he said to everyone at the desk.

Max let out a heavy sigh and stood up. He reached Amy and placed an arm around her waist.

"Brenda...I know I can rely on you to keep Amy safe until I can return to collect her. As she's going to be working here, could you show her the department? Let her get the feel of the place," he asked.

"Of course I will and it will be my pleasure to do so."

Max gave Amy a gentle squeeze and moved away.

"I shouldn't be long," he said.

Walking in Stephanie direction he muttered something beneath his breath which no one heard, and as Max made his exit, Stephanie followed him out of the room.

It was about an hour before Max finally returned to the office to collect Amy.

"I'll take you home to Waterfront but I'm afraid I can't stay," he said, apologetically. "I have to be back at Jordon Towers for a board meeting at six. We're working on the Diablo case this evening and it'll be the only chance I have to brief everyone together before I leave for England next week."

"What?"

There was sudden anger in her voice and before she unleashed the full force of her fury, he pulled her aside into a separate office. The doors were closed making it impossible for anyone to hear what they were saying to one another, but everyone could still see them through the glass partition walls.

They were in full view for all to see.

Amy was thinking that Max had tricked and deceived her. He had made her leave England and he'd brought her to America only to leave her here, trapped in his home, with his child, doing what he wanted her to do.

She would never have uprooted herself and Jake if she'd known what he'd intended to do. She should have held out against Max and stood her ground. She should have stayed in England.

"What's upset you now?" he asked.

"Why couldn't you have left us in England?" Amy said trying not to shout.

"We've been through all that. It was because it will look better if we're seen to be man and wife and you two are living with me as a family in my house."

"But if you're going to be in England. We could have stayed there and you could have stayed with us and..."

"Don't be silly. I have a business to run and it would be impractical. James and I have to thrash out our legal strategy and the best way to do that is if we sit down together in his office in England and go through all the issues and obstacles that might stand in our way."

"But...but I don't know anyone here. I'll be all alone," Amy said. It sounded childish but it was how she felt.

"I'll only be gone a day...two days max." He reached for her and held her close.

She knew it was the most logical solution for Max to travel to England but it didn't stop her from feeling suddenly abandoned.

"Two days?" she whispered against his cheek.

"Promise," he said softly and kissed her brow. "Are you going to be alright?"

It was almost as if he knew what she was thinking.

"I'll be fine. We'll be fine. Jake and I will survive," she said bravely.

"And I thought I was indispensable. It wasn't what I wanted to hear but it will have to do for now. Now let's get you home."

"No...it's alright. You don't have to come with me. You can stay here and finish up. I'll see you this evening when you get home," she said.

He hesitated for a moment.

"You sure?"

"Yes, I'll be fine...really. Only I don't know how I'm going to get home."

"I'll organize the chopper for you." And Max kissed her softly on her lips unaware and blissfully oblivious to the fact that everyone in the outer office was still watching them.

Chapter 9

When Amy arrived back at Waterfront she went to find Jake intending to have some one-on-one time with him before putting him to bed early. It had been a long and tiring day for him and he was exhausted. For once Jake was only too happy to go to his room and sleep.

By nine o'clock that evening Max still hadn't returned from the office and the night was drawing in. Already having eaten her evening meal alone in the dining room, Amy went through to the kitchen to tell Hanna she was taking Max's dogs out for a walk.

"You do that madam," said Hanna. "You'll return relaxed and ready for bed and it will do the dogs some good too. And don't you worry; I'll listen out for master Jake."

It was a kind offer and one that Amy readily accepted.

"Thank you, Hanna."

"You go and have a nice walk with the dogs."

"I haven't had any proper exercise for days and I could do with burning off a few calories."

Since giving birth to Jake, she'd gained a few extra pounds and a few curves in all the right places, but she wasn't overweight. Jake kept her far too busy. Running around after her son all the time, she didn't have a chance to put on weight. She didn't need any diets but she could do with a long vigorous walk.

"Don't you listening to that nonsense, madam. You look fine as you are, and anyway, I once heard master Max say he wouldn't want to live with a bag of bones." Hanna was smiling.

Amy thought of Max and she wondered if that statement would also apply to living with the beautiful, slender Stephanie.

Having collected the dog leashes and after putting Penny and Daniel on their leads, she went out into the night air and headed down towards the beach. The evening was turning cool and she was glad she'd worn her thick, warm, chunky sweater. This was the time of night she loved.

She loved the stillness and silence. The only sounds to be heard were the gentle lapping of the water against the shore or the dogs rustling in the undergrowth.

For nearly an hour she walked along the water's edge and, when the light started to fade, she decided to retrace her steps and return to the safety of the house.

Leaving the dogs in the kitchen she went upstairs to check on Jake. Opening Jake's bedroom door she saw the lamp beside the bed had been left on and as she crossed the room to switch it off Jake stirred in his sleep.

He mumbled something about school and teachers before turning onto his side and drifting off to sleep once again. Quietly she left the room closing the door softly behind her.

She wasn't worried about Jake being upstairs in this big prairie-styled mansion house anymore. Baby alarms had been scattered all over the house and she would hear him should he call out for her.

Returning to the kitchen she saw it had gone eleven o'clock and making sure Penny and Daniel were comfortably bedded down for the night, she made herself a cup of tea and took it along to Max's study to drink. The study was a real man's room with no feminine touches.

She didn't know what pulled her to his room. Maybe it was the heavy, comfortable furniture or the soft sofas dotted about the place, but she chose Max's winged, swivel armchair behind his desk to sit and drink her tea and relax.

Sitting in his chair she thought about the excitement of her day. And in the warmth of the room, her eyes slowly closed and the tea she'd placed on the desk gradually grew cold.

She wasn't aware Max had returned home and found her in his chair with her legs curled beneath her. She was fast asleep and dreaming. He had sat down in the chair opposite. His long legs stretched out in front of him and he'd waited and watched until eventually, she began to stir.

Amy woke with the feeling she wasn't alone in the room and with sleepy eyes she looked up and saw Max sitting across from her.

"You look like you needed that rest," he said. "Why haven't you gone to bed?"

She didn't want to tell him she'd waited up for him because she'd wanted to know he'd got home safely.

Max stood and leant forward gently caressing her check and smoothing a fallen lock of her hair back into place.

She felt the immediate familiar shock of excitement run through her body at his touch.

His gentle caress was electrifying.

"How long have you been sitting there?" she asked.

"Not long," he shrugged carelessly. In truth, it had been nearly an hour.

"You should have gone to bed." She looked at the mantle clock and noticed it had gone midnight.

"I was waiting for you to wake," he explained. "I wanted to claim my kiss."

She looked up at him with a soft, welcoming smile on her lips.

Slowly she stood up from the chair then wished she hadn't. Now she was standing too close to him...dangerously close.

She could feel the heat of his body radiating out towards her. His arms circled her waistline and he held her against the length of him.

"Is Jake still asleep?" she asked.

"Yes. When I got back I went upstairs to see how you and Jake were. I looked in on him and as you weren't in bed I came back down here to find you. I saw the study door open and the light was on."

She was blushing like a self-conscious teenager. It must have looked as if she'd sat up waiting for him to return. Which she had.

Trying to defuse the intensity of the moment she asked, "Would you like something to eat?"

Max gentle placed his hands on her shoulders and began massaging her tenderly.

"No thanks. I don't need something...*to eat*," he whispered softly, nibbling her ear and trailing his lips along the length of her arched neck.

"A coffee?" she tried again.

"No...I need nothing to eat or drink. I only need this...and this." He was softly kissing and devouring her moist lips.

Her eyes closed as his lips pressed against hers.

Time was forgotten as they fused together starved for each other. The kiss went on and on.

As the kiss deepened and hardened, little by little he kissed his way from her lips to her cheekbones and then to her fluttering eyes.

The scent of his aftershave was teasing her nostrils.

It was a fragrant scent that reminded her of sandalwood and cedar trees and it matched his character to perfection. Hard, solid and rugged.

Max gently held and cupped her breasts in his hands. He was arousing her and instantly her nipples were responding to his touch. He was hurting her with pleasure and pain as he awakened her needs.

Her body was beginning to respond. It throbbed and pulsated as he fondled and caressed. It was demanding and craving more than his caresses.

Reluctantly she tore her lips away from his.

"Oh, Max," she whispered.

"What is it my sweet?"

She felt dishevelled and seductively alluring and tingled because Max wanted her.

Unhurriedly Amy trailed the velvety tips of her fingers along his strong masculine jawline and the hard stubble on his jaw rasp her sensitive skin the same way it had scraped the soft skin of her cheek.

Then she found his mouth, and once again their lips met as she invited his tongue to entwine with hers. A reluctant moan escaped from between his open, hungry lips and she felt a deep shudder go through him at her touch.

His kisses were gently seeking. He wanted nothing in return. He was giving, and then his kiss gradually changed, he was taking.

His kisses became deeper, rougher. They had a rawness of longing and urgency.

Amy met him with an equal passion. She was helpless in his hands and he could do with her as he wished.

Abruptly Max lifted his head and his arms were now holding her away from him. He was calling a halt to their lovemaking.

Her breathing came quickly and with her heartbeat pounding and racing violently against her ribs, she waited in anticipation of his next move. But it didn't come.

"I've got some legal briefs for the Diablo trial that I have to read before tomorrow." There was regret in his voice. "James Martin is going to be in touch and I have to be up to speed. I've got to be back in the New York office early tomorrow morning to take his call. I'm sorry..." he said, looking at her longingly.

The sexual tension in her body drained from her. Suddenly she felt let down, deflated and utterly deprived of what she needed.

She needed him.

She wanted Max.

"Oh, don't worry Max. I understand. I understand completely," she said and turning away from him she felt tears of frustration well in her eyes.

Briefly, she wondered if Max had been playing her for all she was worth. Had he made love to her yesterday, took what he wanted from her and was now no longer interested?

The victor had won, the spoils had been claimed, and he had moved on.

The thought was spinning in her head.

"If this meeting with James wasn't so important I would..."

"It's alright Max. You don't need to explain. I understand, truly. There'll be other times when we can..."

"Sure." Max ran a hand in frustration through his dark hair. "I've waited all day to have you to myself and now I've a backlog of work to finish before I can see my bed."

"Then wake me when you come to bed," she told him softly and suggestively, hoping he would still want her.

"Go to bed." He placed a tender kiss on a sensitive spot at the side of her neck. It was a spot he knew excited her. "It'll be a couple of hours before I get to bed and I'll probably be gone before you're awake."

She knew he wouldn't wake her. Not tonight.

"Okay, but if I don't see you before you leave for the city in the morning give my love to James and tell him I miss him," she said.

That was all Max needed to push him over the edge.

He swore heavily beneath his breath before taking her by the hand and pulling her roughly and uncaringly after him up the grand staircase and into their bedroom.

Once in the room he slammed the bedroom door shut and pushed her back against the hard, wooden panels of the door. He held her there with his the weight of his aroused body. His breathing was fast and heavy and she could feel his hot breath blowing fiercely against her cheek.

"We can't do this," she said frantically pulling at his shirt, eager to feel and touch him.

"Sure we can," he said. "Nothing's going to stop me loving you tonight."

"But we shouldn't. You've got work tomorrow and you said James will be calling."

Max leaned heavily against her. It was as if she'd given him a blow and he was defeated before the battle had begun.

"What is it? What's wrong Max?" Something wasn't right.

Then, as if a switch had been turned, his body tensed ready for action.

His mouth found hers and silenced her protests as he brutally plundered her soft, swollen lips.

His hands framed her face and held her.

He was kissing her with such fierce ruthlessness and passion that she could taste blood.

* * * *

Amy was pressed firmly against the cold wood of the door panel and he held her there with his body whilst he devoured her mercilessly and remorselessly. She tasted sweet and he was hungry for more.

His unfounded suspicions of Amy and James had surfaced once more. But this time he wasn't taking any chances. He was going to stake his claim. He was claiming Amy as his procession and she was going to be left in no doubt to whom she belonged. There would be no room in her life for James Martin or any other man for that matter.

"Tell me...what I have done?" she cried.

She wanted to know the reason for his underlying rage. Could she really have no idea why he'd suddenly become so enraged?

He was angry.

"Nothing…you've done nothing," he said.

"Then what is it?"

Jealousy, suspicion and doubt about James tormented him. At their wedding, he'd seen just how close James had been with Amy and he was blindly mistrustful of their relationship.

"Did you have an affair with James?" he asked bluntly.

He had to know. Not knowing the truth was torture. She didn't answer him.

"Did you have an affair with James Martin?" he asked again.

He was holding her roughly by the arms and almost shaking her.

Their bedroom was in darkness lit only by the full moon that was shining through a crack in the curtains. It was difficult to see clearly and he wondered if she could tell he was actually deadly serious in his questions.

"What has James got to do with us?" she asked.

"Nothing...everything," he said trying to make sense of his thoughts.

He was still holding her pinned against the door.

"Well?"

"Well what?" she asked.

The flat of his hand hit the door with such a force that it might have disturbed the whole household. But it didn't. And through gritted teeth, he whispered in her ear.

"You're mine Amy...you'll always be mine."

It was a warning and his meaning was clear. Still holding her tight, the pressure of his hands on her arms wasn't brutal, just forceful.

Even though he had her trembling with fright, to his amazement, she bravely challenged him.

Then she lifted her hand to carefully touch his lips with her fingertips. She was daringly stroking and erotically caressing them before she leant forward to pull and nip gently with her lips and teeth.

"And you Max...are these lips mine or do they belong to Stephanie? Because if they are, I want nothing to do with you."

He sucked in a shocked, deep, sharp breath of horror.

"What did you say? Who's been talking?" he asked angrily.

She couldn't know how much her words had wounded him. He'd hoped to gain something from their marriage. What, he wasn't sure. But he hadn't anticipated that she would reject him so brutally and so totally based on rumours.

He tightened his hold once more.

The torpedo she'd fired in retaliation had hit its target. She'd thrown a wild card into the equation and it had hit its mark.

Did she really think there was something going on between him and Stephanie?

"No one's been talking," she told him. "What is there to talk about? Nothing. Unless the rumours are true? Do your lips belong to Stephanie?"

"Whatever anyone has said or told you, there is nothing between myself and Stephanie. My brother didn't..."

He broke off and didn't complete what he'd been about to say. His head was reeling with thoughts. Thoughts about Stephanie, Brad, Jason, Amy. But he couldn't think about that now. He had to take back control of his thoughts, his mind and his body.

Still holding Amy pinned against the door, he was in a red rage and his hands began tearing, pulling ruthlessly at her clothing.

With cruel speed, he hurriedly began undoing the delicate pearl buttons on her blouse. He was impatient to remove her clothes and in his haste, several buttons were torn away. They fell to the floor and scattered unnoticed into the deep pile of the carpet.

With her blouse discarded, his hands hastily reached behind her to unclip her bra. His deft fingers slipped under her shoulder straps pulling them down over her arms. Once her breasts were freed they fell heavily into his waiting hands.

His mouth hit hers, forcing her lips apart and then she was gasping for air.

His hands covered her breasts cupping their roundness. He lifted them, squeezing them to their full plumpness before capturing a dark, throbbing nipple between his lips. Eagerly he sucked it into his hungry mouth. And as she cradled him against the softness of her swollen breasts, he devoured her.

Amy buried her face against him to hide a sharp agonising gasp of delight she'd felt as he sucked and pulled on her stiff nipples. But he knew of the pain, he knew of the exquisite torture she was feeling because he felt it too.

"Oh, Max," she groaned helplessly.

Hurriedly he groped beneath her skirt lifting it up and around her hips. His hands felt for the lace edging of her panties and he slipped an exploring finger inside her. She was wet and ready for him. Her juices were flowing.

Parting the soft folds of her womanhood with his fingers, he slid his hand along the crack, dipping one long finger deep into her oozing crevice.

He was tormenting her with his finger play.

Gripping her tightly between his finger and the pad of his thumb he rolled and pressed her tender flesh. He was exciting her pulsating, sensitive spot until her legs began to shake and crumble beneath her. Wrapping her arms around his shoulders she clung to him for support.

"Do you want me to stop?" he groaned.

"Uuh…no," she sighed.

He pulled out his wet finger before entering her again with a second. He was stretching her and filling her. She was on tiptoes trying to get away from the erotic torture he was causing, but she couldn't. He held her fast.

"Max..." she groaned wanting more.

His fingers were pumping in and out rasping cruelly against the swollen heat of her sex and she was on the point of coming.

Wasting no time, he tore the remainder of her clothes from her body. He had to have her naked. He wanted nothing to come between them.

The hard buckle of his belt was digging into Amy's flesh and pushing him away, she reached down with trembling fingers, struggling to undo the offending object.

He moaned with need and urgency.

Using both hands, she frantically fumbled with the heavy buckle of his trousers and zipper, and soon they were standing before one another totally naked. Their desire and arousal was apparent.

Lifting her in his arms, he carried her towards the bed and lowered her gently onto it, he stood looking down at her. In the glow of the moonlight, he liked what he saw.

Max Jordan - a billion dollar diamond mogul - a man who could buy anything or have any woman he wanted...wanted only Amy.

She tempts him like no other woman and he was sure that the unbound passion he'd once known and shared with her was still lurking beneath the surface. Every time he touched her something always happened to him. He lost control.

He was no long master of his own destiny. No longer in command. He was a slave to his needs and his need was Amy.

"Amy..." His voice was rough with emotion and longing.

She looked provocative and alluring and he couldn't help but stare at her beauty.

He was amazed and awestruck. He had achieved more than he could have dared wished for. He had brought Amy fighting and kicking to America and once more he had her in his bed. She was lying here beside him and she was his bride.

For years he couldn't forget the way she'd made him feel when they made love...and he still couldn't. She was always with him. The smell of her and the feel of her body were branded in his memory. He hadn't forgotten the exquisite sensations he'd experienced each time he touched her; and although plenty of women had passed transiently through his life since, none had affected him or had power over him, in the same way, that Amy had.

* * * *

The emotion she was feeling for Max was intense and overwhelming. She could never get enough of him. Max had always had that effect on her. He only had to touch her and she would melt. Physically he had power over her.

Lying naked on the bed, and stretching out her arms invitingly, she silently pleaded with him to fulfil her.

She felt the full heavy weight of him as he moved on top. Briefly, he paused, and looking down into her face, his hands began roaming her body knowing instinctively the places to caress and touch. Soon he had her trembling uncontrollably with longing in expectation of what was to happen.

She closed her eyes. To look at him was too painful. The rasping of his body against hers as he moved alongside and his searching hands and embraces were almost too much for her to endure.

She was becoming impatient for the feel of him inside her and impulsively, she climbed over him and straddling his hips, she pinned him to the bed. She couldn't wait any longer and she wanted to push his boundaries. Tonight she didn't want his tender lovemaking. She needed Max to take her with passion and without restraint. But most of all she wanted Max to lose control.

He was a man of power and domination and for once she wanted all his energy focused on her.

Leaning forward she lowered her body until her breasts were brushing back and forth teasingly against the fine dusting of hairs on his chest.

Her hands were stroking his arms, caressing his shoulders lovingly, and then she began to rain light kisses along his jaw, working her way down his torso.

Running her hands down the length of his body she followed the fine hairs to his silky, male tangle. She wriggled down further until she was positioned above him.

His flesh swelled and he stiffened and shuddered beneath her. Max was rigid. He was throbbing and ready...but she waited. She wanted to prolong the moment a little longer.

She could tell he was excited. He wasn't used to someone taking the lead but she sensed he was prepared to let her pleasure him.

Being on top was arousing her and she was exciting herself as much as she was exciting him.

Kneeling above him and positioning him below her, she ran her fingers along the length of his hard, taut shaft and she felt him shudder with need.

"Do it...do it now," he ordered. But she lingered, teasing him with her touch until he could bear it no more.

Impatiently his hands grabbed her hips and buttocks and he pulled her down onto his hard shaft, impaling and penetrating her brutally.

She was ready for him and sinking down onto him, she slid over his full length like a finger of a glove.

Her inner muscles clamped and she was gripping Max to her, holding him fast inside.

For a moment they remained motionless recovering from their onslaught and then slowly and provocatively she began to ride him.

She withdrew and descended inch by inch in rhythmic motions until she was filled. With each withdraw she pulled out and as she reached the tip of his shaft she held him inside her. She didn't quite release him. And then clenching with her inner muscles she went down on him once again holding his rod tightly, squeezing and pumping.

There was a tremendous heat between her legs and he was wet and sticky from her juices. She could feel him throbbing and pulsating with unspent energy.

"How does it feel Max? Do you like it? Do you like this...and this?" She was taking him deep inside her and she wanted to know if she was thrilling him.

She rotated and ground her hips down hard on him until he filled her completely. She felt wanton and sexy and she was revelling in her knew found role.

While his hard, slippery rod was inside her, his fingers were playing in the triangle of soft hair between her thighs. His thumb had found what he sought and he was rubbing firmly on her pulsating clitoris. He was whipping her into an orgasmic frenzy thinking only of her needs and her desires.

She was reaching the heights of her orgasm and she was almost on the point of coming.

And then it came. With a rush of heat, spasm after spasm shook her body. She was filled to capacity and was climaxing before collapsing onto his chest, exhausted.

Max was still engorged and stiff inside her but she didn't care. she was too exhausted.

Her heart was thudding and her blood was pounding in her ears and as they lay entwined together recovering from their lovemaking, she gradually began to stir. She was about to lift herself off of Max's shaft when he stopped her.

"No don't," he told her holding her in position, "Don't move."

He was still erect and deep within her. He needed a release and he needed it soon.

Max wrapped his arms tightly about her and rolling her over onto her back, she was pinned beneath him and still fused together as one.

The pressure and weight of his body were exquisite and she heard Max moan with urgency as he lifted her legs and parted her thighs further. He was opening her fully. Making her ready for his passionate onslaught and then he buried himself deeper and deeper inside her.

His blood engorged rod reached a depth that was sheer torture and yet mind blowing. She was suffering ecstatic torment and she was in delicious pain.

A shock of delight coursed through her body at his brutal touch and as his hands explored and caressed her, there was no kindness in his touch. He was massaging, kneading and possessively fondling her flesh and she was ferociously returning the service. There was no gentleness in her deeds.

Her breasts were swollen and her nipples erect. They were tight and engorged, and when Max cruelly brushed his wet tongue roughly over their peaks there was pain.

With the gentle erotic rasp of his white teeth, he nipped the hard tips of her breasts and sent a womb tingling shock coursing through her. She had no thought of fighting or resisting. She was fully aroused and once again she was on the brink of fulfilment.

Reaching up she held Max's face in her hands and as she returned his embrace, sounds of pure pleasure escaped from deep within her throat. And then Max began his mercilessly pounding into the depths of her. He was relentlessly beating against her womanhood.

Hard, stiff and rigid and he was hitting the very spot that was sending her wild with desire.

Arching her back and lifting her hips she was inviting him in and she wanted to engulf him in her wet cavernous womb.

"No...no," she whimpered. "Max..." It was almost too much to endure.

She was spreadeagled beneath him with her legs parted and her arms above her head, she was open to his invasion.

She wrestled and strained against him but he held her fast as she squirmed beneath him.

His rigid penis was buried deep inside her and then he was pounding remorselessly against her soft inner folds. It was useless to fight his strength. There was no way she could release herself from the savage hold he had on her.

Clasping and locking her firmly to him, Max started his attack. He had her where he wanted her and he began his savage onslaught. He was taking her, grinding into her and beating against her mercilessly and there was nothing she could do about it. This time he was the aggressor and she had to passively accept what he was doing.

She couldn't reach him physically or emotionally. He needed a release and he needed it soon.

There was no sensitivity or feeling in his actions and she suspected she was just a vessel for his use. Then, just when it seemed he would never finish, the mood and tempo of his rhythm changed...and she was instantly excited.

He was now slowly withdrawing and entering her whilst his hand reached down between her legs to rake amongst the soft triangle of hair to find her clitoris.

Rasping and scratching gently between her wet folds with his fingertips he had her bucking against him as she tried to evade the excruciating, yet delightful, painful touch of his seeking fingers.

She had no control over her reflexes as she was skewered and stabbed herself on his hard pulsing rod.

She was nearing orgasm and Max knew it was time. He increased his speed and energy and when he felt her spasms as she clamped down hard on him, he knew she was reaching her peak.

As Max heard her groan of completion, he too discharged and came; gushing and injecting his juices deep into her. Together they had reached the height of orgasm and they collapsed exhausted and spent. But that night there was no satisfying his male hunger.

Max took her again and again. He was ruthless and insatiable and yet tender and aware of her vulnerability.

When they finally finished their fierce passionate lovemaking, she lay aching and bruised next to him. She was trembling and quivering from sheer exhaustion, but she felt complete.

Max reached down and pulled the dishevelled bedclothes over them and nuzzled softly into her neck planting a gentle kiss beside her ear.

"How was it for you?" he asked. His voice was low and husky with desire.

"I love you..." she said in a whisper. "I love you so much."

She didn't dare hope that her love would be reciprocated.

For several minutes she lay nestled in his arms in the aftermath of their lovemaking. Tenderly he was stroking her and soothing her into a calmness and a completeness she hadn't felt in years and she knew she was where she belonged.

Chapter 10

Their days fell into a routine which had pattern and regularity, giving Jake a sense of security and Amy a sense of purpose.

For several weeks Amy had been working with Max at Jordan Towers. She went to the office mainly to help with the Diablo case, but as a newcomer to the team, she'd been making herself useful by generally collecting, sorting and reading relevant data and documents.

The lawsuit had developed to such an extent that Max was constantly travelling back and forth to England. The battle in the courts had been hard going at times, but in the end, they had won.

Having won the case Max's time had been freed up. He could take things easier...and he did.

Weekends he would often take time off from the diamond business to spend quality time with Amy and Jake.

They either stayed together as a family in the New York apartment exploring the city during the day, or they were at home in the Hamptons unwinding. His parents would often join them to relax and dote on their grandchild.

One weekend Alexander and Kim came up from the beach house and were happily spending time with Jake.

"Do you mind if Amy and I disappear for an hour or two?" Max asked them.

"No, of course not," his mother replied. "Where are you off to? Anywhere nice?"

"We won't go far. We're going over to the stables. It's been ages since I've been for a gallop and Amy could do with the practice. She's been having lessons and I'm told she's getting quite good in the saddle. We shouldn't be too long," he said.

"Off you two go. Jake's happy to stay with Grandpa...aren't you Jake? We'll look after him."

Alexander and Kim Jordan were eager to have their grandson to themselves and Max was amazed at how much his father's health had improved since Jake had been in their lives. It was almost as if Alexander and Kim now had something or someone to live for.

"We'll see you all later," Max said, steering Amy out of the room.

Alone in the hall, Max stood towering over her.

"You could have asked me first," she protested looking up at him.

"Why? What were you planning on doing?" he asked.

"Nothing in particular...but that's beside the point. I could have been busy. You assumed I was available," she said slightly irritated.

"Then I assumed right. You are available. So, it seems that for the remainder of the afternoon you're all mine."

"Max Jordan, you're the most self-centred, impossible, egoistic man I have ever met. My only worry is that Jake will turn out to be like his father."

His only response was to take her hand and lead her upstairs in order to change into riding gear before they went over to the stable block.

When they were saddled, ready to ride and on the point of leaving the stables, Amy stopped and looked about her.

"What?" she asked. "No bodyguards? Don't tell me you've given Laurel and Hardy the afternoon off?"

Laurel and Hardy were the nicknames she'd given to the two protection agents that Max constantly had hovering around him. He seldom went anywhere without them and they were usually within easy calling distance.

Except for the times when Max was at Waterfront, the security men were generally glued to his side. Waterfront was the only place where he could let his guard down.

"Like I said, we're not going far and I've got a pager on me should we need to sound the alarm."

"Max you live too much in fear. Now where is it you're taking me this afternoon?" she asked.

Amy skilfully reined in her horse as the frisky mare began to prance.

"If you don't mind, I think we'll head towards the beach. The horses need a good gallop. It will do them good to let off some steam," he said.

Trotting around to the side of the property they reached the wooded area.

"They haven't had a good run in several days and neither have I if it comes to that."

"Do you get much chance to exercise your horses?" She looked at Max's powerful figure as he sat astride his horse, then added, "Not that you need to exercise. You're obviously fit."

"I used to take them out for an early morning run with the dogs but since you've been here my morning schedule has sort of changed. Now the mornings are usually spent exercising in bed." There was a twinkle in his eye as he looked at her. Was he remembering some shared intimate moments?

She knew what he meant. And she felt herself blushed at his words and what he was implying.

She was recalling the type of exercise they had already shared that morning.

"And then there are the school runs you've got me doing. I didn't realise what it would entail when I volunteered to take Jake to school on the way to the airport each morning."

They had arrived at the wooded area and passed through a break in the trees, they reached the sandy beach and the water's edge.

With the first burst of warm weather, people were taking advantage of the sunshine and several small sailboats and surfboards could be seen scuttling against the wind not too far from the shore.

The breeze rippling across the water towards them was cool and she felt herself shiver.

"Are you warm enough?" he asked, seeing her shudder.

"I'm fine thanks. Once we get moving I'll warm up."

From where she was positioned, she could see the beach house where Max's parents lived. It was only a short distance away, but instead of heading towards the house, they turned in the other direction and spurred the horses into a canter along the shoreline. The beach was in a sheltered, secluded cove and everything around them was all part of the Jordan Diamond Empire's private estate.

They'd been riding a while and were enjoying the moment until an outcrop of rock loomed up ahead of them. They had to rein in their mounts.

"That was worth the effort," Max said exhilarated from the exercise. "How was it for you?"

He dismounted and helped her off before walking the horses to cool them.

"Great. But I think held you back," she said.

"No, you didn't. You're a natural."

She was pleased with his compliment. She knew her horsemanship wasn't to his standard but she thought she'd held her own.

They were turning the horses and he was about to help her mount when they heard what seemed to be a cry for help coming from behind the outcrop of rocks. Amy wasn't sure if it had been the wind blowing between the rock and the trees, but Max stood alert, listening.

The cry came again and even with the trees and the rocks obscuring the view, it was obvious someone was in distress.

He passed the reins to her and said, "Tether them and follow when you can." And with that, he ran off along the water's edge clambering over the rocks in the direction of the call.

Having secured both horses to a convenient tree trunk and with her heart pounding in her chest, Amy hurriedly followed in Max's footsteps.

Eventually turning the bend and climbing the rocks she could see what had been concealed behind the line of trees.

A vessel had capsized and was floating in the water. It was leaning on its side at an angle against an outcrop of jagged rocks and she counted three bodies sprawled out on a large massive chunk of rock.

Max stood among them working his way from one body to the next.

With some difficulty, Amy managed to reach the bedraggled group.

There were three very young soaked teenagers. They were wet, dishevelled and obviously in a state of shock.

Max had also been in the water. He was drenched from having dived in to carry one of the teenagers to land and safety.

One of the teenagers was a young girl and she looked to be unconscious. The two boys were in a state of confusion, but they seemed unharmed. Then one of the boys turned onto his side and Amy saw a slash of red running across his back. His T-shirt had been torn.

The ragged edges were smeared with blood and he needed something or someone urgently to stop the bleeding.

Max was busy tending to the unconscious girl. Bent over her, he was supporting her head and performing CPR. Feeling for a pulse and monitoring her breathing he continued to work on the girl even though he wasn't getting a response.

Amy went over to him to see what needed doing.

"Do you want me to help you with the girl or shall I deal with the boy?" She pointed to the young boy who had the back injury.

Max automatically looked to where she was pointing and he saw the blood.

"The boy."

Amy took off her riding jacket saying, "You might need this." And she placed the jacket over the girl to keep her warm before going to see what she could do for the boy.

"Hi, I'm Amy," she said introducing herself. She knelt down beside the young teenager to get a better look at the wound. "I'd like to have a look at your back if that's alright with you."

While she was talking quietly and reassuringly, she was carefully removing the torn fragments of the T-shirt to get a better picture and assess the extent of his injuries.

"You've got quite a nasty gash here. From what I can see it needs cleaning and a few stitches, but as far as I'm concerned I can't see anything major at this moment. The bleeding looks worse than it is," she said trying to put his mind at ease.

She took off her neck scarf and with a torn fragment of his shirt, she made a compression bandage which seemed to stop the flow of blood.

Her talking seemed to reassure him.

The second boy who was with them asked, "How's Ellen? Is she badly hurt?"

Amy looked across at Max. It didn't look good.

"Max is with her," she said. It was all she could think of to say. "What are your names?"

"My name's Aaron," said the boy with the back injury. "And this is Eric; Ellen's brother."

"How did this happen?" Amy asked.

She was trying to take their minds off what was happening.

"We were out sailing," Aaron said. His teeth were chattering as he spoke. "The boat's sail was up and the wind took us with it, driving us onto the rocks."

"Do your parents know where you are?" she asked.

She wished she had some blankets to cover them.

"Yes...no...sort of. We said we were going to the boathouse but I don't think they know we took the boat out," the boy explained.

The boys seemed to be alright although they were both suffering from shock.

Standing up Amy went back over to where Max was. He was still working on the girl.

When she joined him he said, "I don't like it. She's breathing but she hasn't regained consciousness."

He looked worriedly down at Ellen.

"How are the boys?" he asked.

"They're fine. A bit bruised and scratched. One of them will probably need a few stitches but other than that they're doing alright. What would you like me to do?" she asked worriedly.

"I'd like to get this girl to a hospital," he said.

"Shall I ride home and get them to send out an ambulance?"

"No need," he said. "I've called for back-up."

"How did you do that?"

Neither of them had brought their mobile phones with them. They hadn't thought they would need them. Max had left his on the hall table and Amy's was in the bedroom.

He showed her the pager. The pager that was a hotline to his security men and protection. And at that moment all hell broke loose.

From across the water, a chopper could be seen flying in and it was heading straight towards them at high speed. Max had pressed the alarm button and a signal beckon had given their position. It was being transmitted and detected on the chopper's radar.

"Amy...if the boys are alright, do you think you can get to the horses and keep an eye on them? The noise of the chopper is bound to panic them a little," Max asked.

"Sure."

Soon the rescue crew had landed and the three children were airlifted to safety leaving Max and Amy to return home the way they had come.

The security guards were not happy about the situation and they were reluctant to leave Max and Amy on the beach, but Max assured everyone that there hadn't been a threat to his life. And as he always had the final say, the subject was closed for discussion.

They were alone once again and when Max came over to help her into the saddle he paused for a while.

"I don't think you realise how important this moment is for me," he told her quietly letting out a deep sigh. He rested his head against hers.

Running her fingers through his hair she held his face in her hands. She studied him closely and looking deep into his eyes she could see something was distressing him.

"What is it, Max? What's upset you?" she asked.

"A bad memory. But it's nothing. Really. I'm alright," he said.

Gently she reached up and pulled him down to her and as her lips touched his she felt him quiver with desire.

"Amy..."

"What is it, Max?"

"Amy, I need you. I need you to hold me. I need your love."

It was the first time she'd seen him so vulnerable. And then he took her. There in the open, in the seclusion of the cove, with the wind and sea and the waves hitting the shore, he made love to her over and over again like there was no tomorrow.

* * * *

Max and Amy returned to the stables and having handed the horses over to the groom, they went into the house to make a call. Max wanted to see if the teenagers had arrived safely at the hospital.

"You go on upstairs and change," he told her. "I'll make the call and let you know what's happening."

Going up the stairs Amy reached the landing and was about to enter the master suite. The door to Jake's room opened and Kim came out.

"Amy my dear, whatever's the matter? I was with Jake when I heard the noise and commotion of the choppers. Where's Max? What's happened?" she asked showing concern.

"There was an accident on the beach and Max was..." Amy didn't have the chance to say anymore.

"What? He's had an accident?" Kim repeated. "Where is he? How is he?"

Kim looked like she was about to faint.

Amy quickly rushed forward to catch Kim as she stumbled. Helping Kim into the bedroom Amy found a chair and sat her down.

"It's not Max that's been hurt," Amy explained speaking quietly and calmly. "Some teenagers were injured. They needed an ambulance and the chopper's taken them to hospital. Max is alright. He's not been hurt. He's downstairs calling the hospital to find out how they are."

Kim looked relieved. Her son wasn't the one that had been injured.

"I thought the same thing was happening again. I thought Max was..." Kim couldn't speak properly, she was too distraught. "You see his brother had an accident on the beach."

Amy thought she miss heard what Kim had said.

"His...brother?" she said in surprise.

"Yes. Max's twin...Brad. My other son died," she said still shaking.

Kim gave a heart-rendering sob and the tears that fell from her eye were quickly wiped away.

"I didn't realize." Amy could see Kim was very distressed and went to fetch a tissue.

Coming back, she sat down on the bed and waited patiently for Kim to continue.

"It's silly of me to be so upset. But when you mentioned Max and an accident all in one breath, I thought...well, I thought fate had come to claim my other son."

Amy sat patiently and waited for Kim to continue.

"I have two boys...*no*...*I* had two sons. Max *had* a twin brother. When Max and Brad came home to Waterfront for the holidays, Max had his old room and I'd given Brad and Stephanie one of the doubles. They were all in the east wing and Alexander and I were in the west wing. One night something happened between Max and Brad. It had something to do with Stephanie. I don't know what it was about and Max still won't talk about it."

"Perhaps he *can't* talk to you about it," Amy suggested.

"From what I've gathered, Brad stormed out of the house in the middle of the night. He went down to the beach house and Max followed him. But Max was too late. Brad had taken the boat out and he never came back. There was a storm that night and the sea was choppy. The undercurrent swept the boat back to shore and onto the rocks. It was found smashed and wrecked."

"And Brad?" Amy asked.

"Brad's body was found two days later."

"That must have been awful for you...for *all* of you." Amy was shocked to hear what had happened.

She wondered how Max must have felt losing his twin.

"Max was questioned by the police of course, and eventually the result of the coroner's investigation was pronounced. It was given as - *death by misadventure*. Max and Alexander wouldn't let me go to the inquest so I don't know all the facts. Whenever I've questioned Max about that night all he will say is that, *Brad believed what he wanted to believe.*"

"You think Max is protecting you from the awful accident and knowing what had actually happened."

"Yes," Kim said.

"And this afternoon...when I told you about *an accident* you thought Max had been hurt. You thought the worst."

"Yes."

The two women sat quietly for a while thinking about the events of that afternoon and that fateful night.

Eventually, Amy looked at Kim and said, "Max must have been reliving every moment of that dreadful night."

"He's never recovered from the loss of his twin. I loved Brad, we all did and no one can ever replace him, but at least I have one son remaining. Max has lost...a brother. He has lost his twin and I hope never again to see Max as he was on that night. He was a broken man and it looked like the life had been drained out of him."

And at that moment the bedroom door opened and in walked the man they both loved.

* * * *

The days rolled into weeks and the weeks into months.

Several months later, it was the night of Max's thirtieth birthday and Amy was getting ready for the party. The family had decided to hold the event at a grand hotel in New York City. It was to have been a surprise party, but when Max found out about the affair, things were taken out of the family's hands.

He took over organising the event and decided the party was to be held at Waterfront.

Most of the people on the guest list came from his elite social set. His circle of friends and acquaintances were all high fliers. They came from the million dollar income bracket - and if not the million dollar category - then they were ranked as billionaires.

Jake had already been put to bed for the night. He wasn't going to be at the party. It was a formal occasion and not suitable for young children.

Coming out of the shower, wrapped only in a large towel, Amy saw Max was already dressed for the party. He was standing in front of the full-length mirror tying his bow tie. Slipping his watch on and putting his cufflinks into the sleeves of his dress shirt, he stood there looking handsome and very sexy.

It was a black tie affair and his tall, muscular frame suited what he was wearing.

"Shouldn't you be downstairs welcoming your guests?" she asked worriedly.

"*Our guests*...and I thought I'd wait for you." He tweaked the knot and straightened his tie.

"I'm still dressing and they're arriving," she warned. "Someone should be downstairs to greet them."

"Then you'd better hurry," he said.

Amy dived into a dresser drawer and pulled out some underwear. There was a slight panic in her voice. She'd been delayed from getting ready and was running behind schedule. Jake had sensed something big and exciting was happening and she had stayed with him a while, wanting to reassure him that everything was fine.

"Which do you prefer?" she asked showing Max the two gowns she'd chosen for the occasion. "The black or the white?"

"That depends. Which gown would you prefer to wear with these?"

Max went over to a table and picked up a jewel case. Opening the box he showed her a diamond and ruby necklace with a matching ring.

She had come to learn that she was a show case for his jewels. He gave her jewellery all the time. Some he told her to keep and others - when she had worn them - were returned to the vaults at Jordan Towers.

It felt strange keeping his priceless jewels amongst her precious trinkets.

"They're beautiful," she told him truthfully, but she dreaded having to wear such a magnificent set of stones.

Inevitably at any event she went to with Max, all eyes would turn to her to make an assessment. They all wanted to know the name of her dress designer. But more importantly, they wanted to see her jewels.

"It's going to have to be the black;" she said thoughtfully. "That deep red ruby will go with the black. Is that alright?"

"Fine. Now hurry," he said trying to speed her up.

Amy went back into the dressing room and hastily returned the white set of underwear and selected a black satin stocking bodice.

The corset was fine boned and had a lace trim.

Sexy wasn't the word for it. When she'd discarded her towel and was dressed in the laced underwear and stockings, she returned to the bedroom where she'd left the gown and started to dress.

Max had taken off his evening jacket and was laid back on the bed patiently waiting. He was looking at her admiringly.

Stepping into her black high heel and turning to find the evening dress, she heard Max leave the bed. He came and stood behind her.

Circling his arms around her he pulled her back against him. One of his hands cupped her full rounded breast whilst the other reached down to touch the bare expanse of skin showing between her stocking tops and the corset.

Unknowingly she had been arousing him.

Seeing her provocatively dressed in only her underwear had stirred his blood and it seemed he couldn't resist...he had to feel her. Lowering his head, he nuzzled into the curve of her neck planting a trail of light kisses along the bareness of her shoulders.

"Max...we've got to get ready. Let me finish dressing," she said as she leant provocatively against him.

"In a moment."

He was feeling her and his hands were moving over her, but he couldn't feel what he wanted to feel. Although the silk corset was barely covering her flesh, it was protecting her from his searching hands and she heard his frustration.

It was almost as if she was wearing an armoured breast plate. His sexual arousal was growing and she knew he had to have her...now.

His hand found a way into her silk panties and his fingers sought and found her throbbing clitoris. He was gently massaging and rubbing her until it was her turn to squirm and wriggle in torment.

Amy turned to face him and threw her arms around his neck. She was holding on to him in case she should fall. And then he was kissing her. Biting on her soft, lower lip and then he was pushing his fingers wet from her juices deep inside her.

"We have to stop," she cried.

But he wasn't listening.

He pulled her panties down as far as he could and, unzipping his trousers, he released the pressure on his stiff, rigid rod. He took her savagely exactly where she was standing.

It was a quick release of their sexual desires for both of them and it had been unsatisfying, but neither of them cared. They knew they would have the full passion of their lovemaking later that night.

Chapter 11

Downstairs the house was buzzing and filling with people. Guests from all over the world were being flown into East Hampton Airport where they were then ferried to Waterfront in long, sleek, black limousines.

Amy had mentioned to Max that she would feel out of her depth among all these strangers, but he'd reassured her that she wouldn't feel alone. There would be several of her friends there.

Some of the people she had come to know since she'd moved to America were coming this evening - people like Frank and people like Brenda and her husband - so at least she would have a few friendly faces to talk to.

Kim and Alexander were also going to be at the party and of course, James had arrived from England. James was staying in New York City with Cathy and they were travelling to the Hamptons tonight for the party.

Even so, Amy was daunted by the prospect of meeting and hosting such a grand event for so many wealthy and powerful people.

Max eventually decided it was best if he went downstairs to greet their guests leaving Amy to finish dressing.

The black evening dress had a high, round neckline and a deep, plunging, open back. Having the swirling skirt brush against her legs gave her a very sensual feeling and she wished Max was here with her now. Their short skirmish had left her wanting more.

Carefully she redid her makeup and splashed some perfume on the pulse points at her wrists and neck.

When she was ready she went downstairs to look in on the caterers. She needed to check that the last minute finishes had been done and that everything was going according to plan.

Earlier that day several of the large, whitewashed outbuildings surrounding the house had been made ready for the party and all sorts of activities had been planned for their guests. In one building a dance floor had been laid down and a band had been hired to play. In another, a refreshment tent had been set up.

No expense was being spared. Max was entertaining on a grand and lavish scale.

Having checked in on the staff, Amy went through to the drawing room where she found Max drinking a whisky. He was waiting for her and he hadn't yet seen her enter the room. Stood in front of the burning fire he had his back towards her.

Through the open French windows, the sound of the music could be heard coming from the party. It was drifting in on the warm evening breeze and the curtains seemed to be swaying in time to the beat.

"Max."

He turned at the sound of her voice and saw her coming towards him.

"At last... Shall we go and meet our guests? Let's see what the evening has in store for us?" he said.

She didn't answer him. Instead, she came to a stop in front of him and held out her hands. She was holding two beautifully wrapped packages.

"For me?" he asked.

"Happy birthday Max."

She reached up and gave him a kiss, but before the kiss could deepen she pulled away. She knew that if their emotions got out of hand they would never make it to the party.

Max placed one of the presents on a nearby table and began to remove the wrapping on the other. He revealed a man's silver pocket watch and chain.

It wasn't the usual type of watch he wore but she'd thought it was an unusual and original gift and hoped Max might like to wear it when he was dressed in his three-piece suits.

"It looks lovely," he said.

He held the watch away from him to admire it and then, taking a closer look, he saw there was an inscription on the back.

To Max - My Husband - The Clock is Ticking.

It was a reminder of a time in England when she'd told him she was his for six months. It had been a time when she'd said that she considered their wedding and marriage a temporary business arrangement.

Max looked as if he'd been given a slapped in the face. As if he'd had a reality check.

"The clock is ticking. What are you trying to tell me, Amy? That you're moving on and going back to England and taking our son with you? I know I told you I had to *be married and stay married* until I was thirty...but what are you telling me? That our time together has run out? What?" he said in frustration.

Max looked devastated by the words he'd just read on the watch.

"Max..." she was alarmed and amazed by his reaction.

"I should never have trusted you," he said bitingly. "And I should never have let James come to America for the party. I haven't seen him yet but I presume he's somewhere in New York waiting for you. Have you been seeing him behind my back?" he growled.

"Max you're taking this the wrong way." She was pleading with him, wanting to explain. "James has nothing to do with this."

At some point earlier in the week Max had been feeling generous and he'd phoned England inviting James to the birthday party. James had dropped everything and he'd cleared his work schedule arranging to fly into New York City early for the celebrations.

"Have you seen James?" he asked her again and his teeth were clenched tightly together. His anger and pain were unmistakable and plain to see.

"Yes...I've seen James. We had lunch *together* yesterday," she said.

She didn't tell Max she'd had lunch with James and Cathy Moore.

Working together in the London office Cathy and James had recently struck up a friendship and things had developed to such an extent that they had become engaged. The two of them had decided to combine Max's party in the Hamptons with a long, romantic weekend break in New York.

"Who gave you permission to see James? You're mine," he said glaring at her.

Max sounded like Jake. Demanding, childish and possessive.

Jake had gone through a phase where he'd been very selfish of his toys and belongings, and it appeared that Max had the same trait.

Max pulled Amy hard up against his body and capturing her left hand in his hand.

He showed her the rings he had put there.

She was amazed at the nerve of the man. Who did he think he was and what right did he have to dictate to her who she could or could not see?

"Max Jordan, if you think you have exclusive rights over me or what I do, then you don't know me," she said.

"I know that you belong to me and I always keep what I have."

His sudden and brutal kiss was savagely vicious. There was unrestrained anger as he took what he wanted and claimed what he thought was his and his alone.

"James and I..."

Once more he kissed her, silencing her cruelly with his mouth.

"No, don't bother explaining," he said. "Your message is coming over loud and clear. It's a shame because for a while I thought we had something going for us. I thought we could make a go of our *temporary* marriage, but obviously, I've been mistaken. Six months you promised me and I was prepared to wait six months for you. But now it seems our marriage is unnecessary. You can leave. Go...go now. Go back to England and go back to James. I'm releasing you from our agreement," he said angrily.

"I don't understand. What do you mean?"

"The deal's off. You're no longer needed."

His words were harsh and cruel.

"But what about our marriage? We have to stay married or you'll lose the company," she said desperately.

"That *was true,* but things have changed. If you recall I had two options. I had to marry before I was thirty and remain with my wife or I had to find some more shares from somewhere to gain control of the company."

"That was the reason we married."

"But it's no longer the reason why we have to *stay* married, *my love.*" There was no shred of tenderness in his voice. There was only derision and anger in his voice when he had called her his love.

"This weekend I'm celebrating my thirtieth birthday and my mother has given me a very generous birthday present. She's given me her shares in the company. That means I'm now the major shareholder and I've total control of the company. It also means that we don't have to stay married...so you can go. I'm giving you permission to go back to James."

She couldn't believe what she was hearing.

"*The clock is ticking...*" he said.

He was dismissing her as if she was of no consequence. In essence, he was telling her he no longer had a use for her.

"So it was always about the shares and the company," she said, feeling wounded beyond belief. "It was never about the two of us. Five years ago I was in the same position I'm in now and look what happened then...you dropped me. When you got to America and got the partnership in the law office you finished with me and now it's happening again. You get what you want and then you move on. You've never loved me have you Max? You've only used me and I should have known better. I mean nothing to you, do I?"

Max had turned a deathly pale colour and looked as if Amy had stabbed him and torn his heart out. He didn't say anything and he didn't deny her accusations.

"What about Jake?" she asked. "Do you want to visit him in England or do you want to sever all contact. It's a shame because he's grown extremely attached to Kim and Alexander."

"Jake stays here. There's no question of you taking him with you when you leave," he said viciously.

Amy swallowed hard and clenched her fists into a ball.

"I'm not leaving Jake with you Max. You might think you can have him but..."

"Jake is my son and he stays with me."

"And I'm his mother."

"Then you'll have to choose. Jake or James. You can stay here with Jake and we'll live separate lives or you can leave with James and never return. I'd prefer it if you left. But it's your choice. Jake or James?"

Running his hands savagely through his dark hair Max took one last disdainful look at Amy before storming across to the open French windows and walking out into the darkness of the night.

He left without a backward glance and he headed for his waiting guests in the sprawling outbuildings behind the house.

Max had given her an ultimatum and she knew she had to make a decision. She had to decide to stay with Max knowing he didn't love her or leave...without Jake.

There was no question in her mind Max wouldn't play fair regarding parental rights and visitation. He would probably only allow her to have Jake during the long summer holidays but she wasn't going to relinquish her rights on Jake. She had too much to lose.

At this moment Max was in a blind rage. He was ranting and raving and no amount of rational reasoning would have an effect on him.

Amy stood rooted to the spot quivering and trembling uncontrollably from the emotional onslaught she'd just endured. She was physically unable to move. And then she saw the discarded presents she'd given him on the table in front of her and her eyes filled with unshed tears.

He hadn't given her a chance to explain about the silver pocket watch with its inscription and he hadn't looked at his other unopened present; the one she had chosen with such care.

Silently she was choking back her tears.

The unopened gift was a chunky personalised gold key-ring with a key shaped disc attached. She'd had both presents specially commissioned for his birthday.

It was a gold key-ring and a gold key that wouldn't open any doors. Inside the disc was a miniature photo of Jake and herself and an inscription which read - *'you hold the key to our hearts.'*

It was a trinket. A talisman. It was something he could carry with him wherever he went in the world and it would be there to remind him of them.

The uncut key had no practical use for the man who had everything, but it would symbolise and hold all the love she had to give.

But he hadn't opened the present and he hadn't seen their photos.

She couldn't stay here much longer. Max had more or less said she was no longer welcome in his home. He had told her to leave but she couldn't leave...not in the middle of the night and not without Jake.

Although she felt on the point of collapse, she knew she would have to go and pack the few belonging they had brought with them from England. Not being able to face Max and the party she thought she might as well make a start now.

She couldn't and wouldn't take anything Max had given her and the sooner she and Jake were packed and ready to leave the better.

Heading towards the staircase and with her eyes full of tears, she walked unseeingly straight into Frank. He had come in search of her. Max had sent Frank to find her and to bring her to the party.

Frank caught and held Amy as she stumbled and nearly fell.

"Hey steady. No so fast." Seeing Amy was distressed and overwrought he asked, "Are you alright?"

"Sorry, Frank. I didn't see you there," she said.

Quickly she wiped away her tears with the back of her hand.

"What is it? What's wrong?"

"Nothing. I'm alright. I'm fine...really. If you'll excuse me Frank, I have to go upstairs."

She had to get away. She didn't want Frank to see how upset she was.

"Max sent me over to collect you. He said I was to stay with you and under no circumstances was I to leave you. I'm here to escort you to the party," Frank explained.

"I'm sorry but I won't be going," she told him apologetically, but she didn't tell him the reason why.

"I hate to contradict you but...*you are*," he said.

Frank was using a tone of voice she'd never heard him use before. He was always a happy-go-lucky type of guy, but tonight he was a man on a mission and he wasn't taking no for an answer.

"But..."

"Amy, with the mood Max is in, it's more than my job's worth to disobey him," he said.

Amy realised her husband was on the war path. Max was out to get her and he was trying to rein her in and break her spirit. He was issuing restrictions and taking control, and Frank was an innocent tool being sent to do the dirty work.

She couldn't blame Frank. He was only the messenger.

"Okay. I'll just go and freshen up and I'll join you at the party as soon as I'm ready."

She felt defeated. Max had everything going for him. He even had Frank doing the dirty work.

"It's alright, I'll wait."

"Where's Max now and why couldn't he come to get me himself if he wanted me so urgently?" she asked infuriated by the whole situation.

"I left him with Stephanie. They're—"

Hearing Max and Stephanie's name coupled together was the last straw.

"No stop," she said vehemently. "I don't want to hear about Max and Stephanie. It's none my business who Max chooses to spend his time with...not now."

Max had gone straight from her arms to find Stephanie.

Briefly, she wondered if he'd planned to be with Stephanie right from the beginning. If he wanted to be with Stephanie, why hadn't he married his brother's wife in the first place? But even as she began to think

Max had married her as a cover up to something more sinister, she realised it couldn't be true.

Max was respectful of the law and she knew the man she loved would never do anything unlawful. He would always do the right thing.

"Max and Stephanie being together isn't what it seems," Frank tried to tell her.

Frank was obviously worried that he'd inadvertently said something that he shouldn't have. He'd heard the panic in her voice and he wanted to reassure her that everything was fine.

"Leave it Frank."

Amy didn't want to talk about it any longer. The subject was too sensitive and she was too raw with emotion.

Reluctantly she went upstairs to repair her ruined makeup and when she came back down she allowed Frank to escort her to the party.

She knew that ultimately, sooner or later, she would have to attend. It couldn't be avoided. It was her duty as hostess to be there and as a Jordan, she had to do what was expected of her.

When they reached the outbuildings Frank took her inside and they looked about trying to locate Max.

"I left Max over there," he said, pointing to a corner where a drink's bar had been setup.

The place was full of elegant people dressed in evening suits and glittering gowns and they were either sat at tables or mingling in the crowd. Amy recognised none of them. They were all Max's friends or business associates and they were all strangers to her.

She was beginning to feel out of her depth and her insecurities about being in his elite world were beginning to surface again.

"I can't see him, can you?" She was looking about and searching, but there was still no sign of Max.

Then Frank spotted Alexander and Kim on the other side of the room and steering Amy over to their table he asked if they knew where Max was.

"We're looking for Max," he explained as he greeted Kim with a kiss on both cheeks. "You haven't seen him by any chance?"

Kim and Alexander both shrugged their shoulders and shook their heads.

"Not recently," Alexander answered. "He's probably circulating. Doing the rounds. Have you tried looking in one of the other buildings?"

"Not yet but we'll do that now. Thanks a lot, sir." Frank gave Kim another kiss and shook hands with Alexander. "We'll catch you later if we get a chance."

"We won't be here," Alexander warned. "I'm taking Kim back to the beach house. We've been holding the fort for a while and I think we've done our share of diplomatic duty. We'll let you younger ones take over."

Amy had difficulty making eye contact with Kim and Alexander. She couldn't look at the two people she had come to like and respect - and love - knowing she would be leaving them soon.

"I'll bring Jake over to see you tomorrow as promised." Amy was speaking to Kim. "It's kind of you to have him. With Max having invited a few friends to stay at the house tonight it will be easier for everyone if Jake's out from under our feet. Not that he's a problem, he never is. And I'm sure he'll love having quality time with his grandparents."

She would have to tell Kim and Alexander that she was leaving Max sometime but she couldn't tell them now. Not this evening. Now wasn't the right time or the right place to reveal that Max had more or less kicked her out of the house.

No, she simply couldn't tell them. Not at this party and certainly not in front of all these guests.

Once again Amy and Frank said their goodbyes and making their way outside they went into the next building in search of Max.

The throbbing beat of the music was sounding out into the night and the glittering lights of the disco were casting shadows around the room. And then she saw him. He was looking directly at her from across the room.

Max saw her stiffen. He was aware she was there but he had made no move to come to her.

Then the woman standing beside him caught and held his hand. It was Stephanie. In a provocative manner, Stephanie began pulling Max behind her as they headed onto the dance floor.

Max hadn't protested and he hadn't resisted.

He was entwined and swaying to the music with Stephanie in his arms and they were pressed body to body with no room to spare.

Amy couldn't look at the two of them together any longer. It was unbearable.

She felt a tightening in her chest as if Max was crushing and breaking her heart and she had to turn away. But as if drawn to the horror of what she was seeing, her tormented eyes returned to the couple like a moth to a flame.

"It's not what it seems," Frank said, vehemently.

He was endeavouring to reassure her that what she was witnessing wasn't real. Quickly Frank began pulling her away. He was trying to block her view and to stop her from seeing what looked like a passionate clinch.

"And how is it supposed to seem?" Amy asked on a sob.

"It's probably a birthday kiss. I know for certain Max is totally committed to you. He's told me he is."

"And he's so committed to me that he's in the arms of another woman. I might be a fool, Frank, but I wasn't born yesterday," she said.

"But they're only dancing."

"Yes, dancing and much more. Frank, I'm not blind. My eyes aren't deceiving me. And from what

I've seen, Max doesn't exactly seem to be fighting Stephanie off."

Frank navigated Amy away from the crowds until she was out of sight of Max and Stephanie entangled on the dance floor.

They walked out into the cool of the night and headed toward the main house away from the noise of the party.

"Max wouldn't touch Stephanie with a barge pole. I know it," Frank said, steadfastly defending his friend.

"And I know differently. Not everyone knows I'm Max's wife, and during the months I've been working at Jordan Towers, I've heard the gossip about Max and Stephanie. The gossip's rife. It's been going around the office. I've given Max the benefit of the doubt but I can't take it anymore...I can't. What am I supposed to do? Turn a blind eye to his affair?"

"Affair? What affair?"

"The affair my husband's having with his sister-in-law," she answered.

having reached the house, they were on the veranda and Frank took her arm, steering her to one of the many rattan chairs. He made her sit.

"Stop, Amy. Stop before you say something you'll regret."

"But I heard someone at the office say Stephanie had been found in Max's bed the night Brad died.

And for some reason, Max and Stephanie both went to England together and..."

It was torturing her to think of the horrid things she was told concerning Max and Stephanie.

"Of course Stephanie had to go to England," Frank said. "She had to testify in court. Stephanie was the one who gave Diablo access to the stolen diamonds. She couldn't refuse to go. She'd been subpoenaed," he explained.

"But...but...the night Brad died..."

"Max loved his brother and he wouldn't have done anything to jeopardise that relationship. I wasn't at the inquest to hear all the gory details but I saw Max during that time and I saw the hate he had for Stephanie. No, there was never anything between Max and Brad's wife. There wasn't anything then and there isn't anything now. I'd bet everything I own on it."

Staying on the veranda, Frank and Amy talked for a while longer and all the time Frank was trying to convince her leaving Max was a wrong move. But Amy had made her decision and she was on the point of going into the house to collect Jake and pack their bags, when Kim and Alexander could be seen approaching the house.

Frank enlisted their help and Amy was forced to tell all.

She told about the arranged marriage and the reason Max had married her in the first place. Then she confessed to them what had happened earlier that evening.

"He said I didn't have to stay with him any longer because he now has all the shares he needs to control the company. He doesn't need me and he doesn't love me," she said as her eyes slowly began to fill with tears.

Kim heard the hurt in Amy's voice.

"Of course he does. I've seen the way he looks at you and there's no doubt in my mind that my son loves you," she said taking Amy's hand.

"It's no good, I can't take any more. Especially after what was said to me this evening. I have to leave him...now...tonight. I'm going to pack our bags and I'm taking Jake and we're leaving on the next available plane. We're out of here.

"Stay and talk to Max," Kim said trying to persuade her.

"It's no good. Max wants to keep Jake and he wants me to leave with James," Amy said.

It took Kim all of two minute to sum up the situation and offer a solution.

"Go and wake Jake and bring him to the beach house. You can stay with us tonight and after you've slept on it we'll talk in the morning when you're not so upset."

Eventually, and with some reluctance, Amy was persuaded to do as Kim suggested. With Frank aiding and abetting the departure from Waterfront to the beach house, he helped collect their belongings and carry a sleepy Jake over to the house.

"Do you realise I won't be able to show my face again at the party?" Frank asked with trepidation in his voice. "If Max finds out that I know where his wife and Jake are hiding out he won't let me survive."

"Then you'll have to fly back to Toronto tonight and keep a low profile," Alexander warned. "After we've finished here you can take the chopper to the airport and I'll order the jet to be on standby for you."

Amy saw a light at the end of the tunnel when the plane was mentioned. The jet would offer her a possibility and a chance of escape.

"Wouldn't it be easier for everyone if Jake and I took the jet and left America tonight?" she asked.

"*No*," was the resounding unanimous vote from the three people beside her.

Chapter 12

It was nearing two o'clock in the morning and it wasn't until most of the guests had left the party that Max had the opportunity to start looking around for Amy. He'd assumed that having seen him on the dance floor with Stephanie she'd gone back to the house in a tiff. But when he went in search of her and discovered their bedroom was empty and Jake had gone, his pulse rate soared and heads started rolling.

Amy had vanished.

It was as if she had disappeared from the face of the earth taking Jake with her.

His personal bodyguards and Jordan security were dispatched but no evidence of Amy and Jake's whereabouts could be found.

The usually decisive Max was at a standstill and he didn't know which way to turn.

Leaving the chaos of the house he went outside and stood alone on the veranda listening to the sounds of the night.

Somewhere in the distance car doors could be heard slamming and there were shouts of farewells being called out as guests said their goodbyes to one another. It was then that Max saw James Martin coming towards him from across the lawn.

He wasn't alone. There was a woman with him and for one heart-stopping moment, Max thought it was Amy. It did matter that she was with James. All that mattered was that she was safe and unharmed. But it wasn't Amy.

James hadn't seen Max at the party. It had been such a large gathering and there had been so many people present that not everyone had had the chance to see Max to personally wish him a happy birthday.

Seeing Max standing on the veranda, James was coming over to say goodnight to his host before leaving.

"A great evening Max. I've never been to a better party but what's happened to Amy?"

James was holding out his hand for his friend to shake but Max was oblivious to the friendly overture. All Max saw was the man whom he thought had taken Amy away from him and he wanted to lash out and swing his fist into James's face.

Max, who had never struck anyone in anger before, was fighting the urge to floor James and knock him to the ground.

"Where is she? What have you done with my wife? And where's my son?"

"Hey, now hold on a minute. What are you on about?"

James had no idea what the problem was or what was causing Max to behave in such a hostile manner. Max was oozing aggression and James could feel the full onslaught of the fury being directed towards him.

"Amy. What have you done with her?" Max was seeing red and he was ready to explode.

Recovering from the unexpected verbal onslaught received only seconds ago, James loosened his tie and shrugged his shoulders non-plus.

"We haven't seen Amy all night," he explained. "Cathy and I are just about to leave. We thought we'd come over and say goodbye. We haven't seen Amy since yesterday," he said.

"What do you mean you haven't seen her?" Max was baffled by the whole situation and looked as if he was about to attack.

Cathy stepped forward.

"We haven't seen her, at least not tonight. Max, what is it? What's wrong?"

There was deep concern in Cathy's voice and she looked worriedly at Max.

"Is Amy missing?" she asked.

And then it suddenly dawned on Max that Cathy was here...and she was with James.

"Cathy? What are you doing here?" He was confused by her presence. "You ought to be in England. Why are you in America?"

"I'm here with James of course," she said.

"Does Amy know?" Max asked.

"Does Amy know what? That I'm here with James? Of course she does. We all had lunch together yesterday. Didn't she tell you? Max, what's wrong?"

Max slumped down on the veranda steps and put his head in his hands. He looked like a broken man. He had accused Amy of having done some dreadful things and whilst he'd been berating her, she hadn't defended herself against his ferocious and merciless onslaught of accusations.

Explaining to James and Cathy what had happened that evening wasn't easy for Max. But he did confess. And in doing so he came to realise what a fool he'd been.

After James and Cathy left, Max went back into the empty house. He felt totally alone.

Wandering from room to room there was no sign of Amy or Jake, or them ever having been there. Their personal things had gone and it was as if she'd erased their very existence.

And then he saw something Amy had given him on one of the side tables in the drawing room. It was his birthday present. It was the pocket-watch that had caused so much distress to them both.

Holding it in his hand, once again he looked at the inscription she'd had engraved - *To Max - My Husband - The Clock is Ticking* - and it felt like a lifetime had passed since he'd last seen her.

Carefully he slipped the watch into his pocket.

He still had something of hers. She was still with him.

* * * *

Two days had passed since the party and there had been no word or sign from Amy. There had been nothing...only silence. It was as if Amy and Jake had somehow vanished into thin air.

The airports had been checked for departures and Max had questioned everyone he could think of, but he'd had no luck.

There was no record of Amy or Jake having left the country.

The only other possibility that sprung to mind was that she might have found someone at the party to take her out of the country and away from him.

Being a man accustomed to action, waiting and doing nothing was torture for him. Eventually, he made the decision to fly to the London townhouse knowing that she thought of it as her home. It would be a safe bolt hole for her to run to, but when he arrived in London she wasn't there and the house was still boarded up and empty.

He knew she couldn't have gone far.

She was a woman alone and she had a child in tow. At some point, the authorities would come across her in the system and she couldn't hide from him indefinitely because she had nowhere to hide.

A week passed and totally defeated Max flew back to the Hamptons intending to wait it out and see where she surfaced. Walking into Waterfront he immediately saw an assortment of luggage standing in the hallway and recognised it as belonging to Amy. But there was no one to be seen.

"What's happening?" he called out into the emptiness of the echoing hallway. He was demanding to know the meaning of what he was looking at, but no one answered.

No one appeared and no one replied.

He stood with his hand on his hips viewing the chaos of luggage strewn about him.

"Have I not made myself clear?" he shouted. "What is happening here?"

He had raised his voice and was looking furiously about him.

"Well?"

The door to the drawing room opened slowly. Kim stood staring at her son, amazed at his dictatorial behaviour.

"Hello mother," he said as if it was the most natural thing in the world for him to find Kim in his home.

He bent to place an affectionate kiss on her cheek and entered the drawing room where he saw his father seated beside a roaring fire drinking a coffee and reading the papers.

"I hope you two have been making yourselves at home in my house whilst I've been away. Where's Amy?" he demanded.

Alexander put down the paper he was reading.

"You do not talk to us, and especially to your mother, with that tone of voice my boy," Alexander said with firmness in his voice.

"No, sir. You're absolutely right, sir. My apologies."

Max, a man of the world and master of all he owned, had been justly and rightly reprimanded.

"Amy's not here," Kim replied.

Suddenly the life seemed to drain out of Max. His face turned ashen and his hands fell limp to his sides.

Kim had only ever seen that look on Max's face once before and that was on the night his brother disappeared.

The thought of torturing Max a little longer for the anxiety he'd put Amy through vanished when Kim saw the pain her son was in. But before she could tell Max where Amy was, Jake appeared.

From upstairs in his bedroom, Jake had heard the sound of his father's voice and had come running downstairs bursting into the drawing room.

"Daddy...daddy...where have you been?" he cried excitedly.

Bending down Max opened his arms and lifted Jake up to face him square on. He planted a generous kiss on his son's head.

Overcome by emotion Max gave Jake another warm, gigantic bear hug before setting him down on his feet.

"Ouch, you're hurting me, daddy," squealed Jake.

"Not as much as you've hurt me this week. I've missed you."

There was a suspicion of a tear in Max's eye as he looked at his son.

"And mummy and me have missed you. Mummy's been crying and crying and we've really missed you."

"Do you know where mummy is?" There was anxiety and apprehension in Max's voice. He didn't know if he could bear to hear the worst.

Seeing the torment in Max's eyes Kim couldn't take it any longer. She had to put him out of his misery. Kim pulled Max to one side until they were out of earshot of Jake who had gone to sit with his grandfather.

"Amy had to get out of the house for a while. She didn't want Jake to see her in the state she was in so she went down to the beach."

Kim saw Max visible relax. Amy wasn't out of reach. He could still find her and persuade her and...

"Amy and Jake have been staying with us since the party and Amy's letting Jake stay with us a little longer," Kim explained softly. "That's why she's been so upset."

"What do you mean Jake's staying? What about Amy?" he asked.

"Max...Amy's made a decision. She wants to leave. We've tried to persuade her not to go but she won't listen to us. She said you told her to go and..."

"She's leaving...for England? And she's not taking Jake with her?" Max asked in disbelief.

"Max, you must have really hurt her with the things you said. Nothing anyone has said to her can make her change her mind. She's due to depart in an hour."

It seems as if he had found her only to lose her again.

"She's on the beach. If you hurry..." Kim said.

That was all the warning Max needed and he rushed towards the door and was gone.

* * * *

Amy had left Alexander, Kim and Jake at the main house and she'd gone to the beach to clear her head.

She had to think.

Leaving Jake and everyone she had come to love in America wasn't easy. It was the hardest decision of her life and she needed time to come to terms with it. But she didn't have time. She knew she had to make a clean getaway before Max found her. She couldn't face his onslaught of accusations again.

She thought he knew how much she loved him but obviously, he didn't.

How could he possibly believe she would share his bed, giving him everything she had to offer, and then accuse her of wanting to be with James?

She hadn't understood it then and she couldn't understand it now.

The heat of the day was still lingering in the evening air and as she strolled back along the shore she started to feel calmer.

And then she saw him.

He was casually dressed. He was wearing beige chinos with an open-necked shirt and casual loafers. His powerful strides were bringing him closer towards her and, as usual, his hands were trust deep into his trouser pockets. He looked totally out of place on the beach dressed as he was, but she didn't care.

She felt her heart skip and lurch at the sight of him. Her breath caught in her throat and there was no denying the attraction she was feeling.

And then the horror of the party came back to haunt her.

She waited for him to join her at the water's edge and when he did, Max simply wrapped his arms about her holding her close. He was holding her as if he would never let her go.

Calmly, as if was the right place to be, she buried her head against his broad shoulder. She was where she belonged. She was with Max.

Silently they stood together and with their arms wrapped around each other, they looked out over the great expanse of water watching the sun as it began to set.

"Hello *my Amy,*" he said tenderly.

It felt as if he had come home.

Max was staring at her intensely and his eyes were boring and penetrating deep into her innermost being.

"Why do you look at me like that?" she asked. She was peering up at him in the fast fading light.

"How am I looking at you, my love?" he asked.

"I don't know. It's like..."

"It's because I am happy and I adore you," he said simply.

"Then I like how you look."

His hands reached for her face and he planted soft gentle kisses on her temple. His tender caress meant more to her at that moment than any of the passionate lovemaking which had gone before.

Gradually they began to make their way back to the beach house and Max steered her towards a cushioned bench on the veranda.

"I think its question and answer time, don't you?" he said. Putting his arm around her, he pulled her close against his side.

She nodded soundlessly in agreement.

As she buried her face shyly against him there was the familiar smell of his masculine scent mingling with a cedarwood aftershave. She felt at peace.

"You start," he told her.

She didn't know where to begin but she knew she had to.

"Stephanie...I saw you with her on the night of the party," she said.

"And I saw you and I wanted to make you jealous. Stephanie was coming on to me and before I could stop her she was giving me a birthday kiss. That was all it was. A kiss. But when I saw your reaction it made me feel I had committed the worst sin ever. And I had. It was a betrayal. A betrayal of us and what we *have,*" he explained.

"But you had been with her before that night." She was half-heartedly accusing him of something she didn't want to believe was true. She hoped he would refute what she'd just accused him of...and he did.

"No never," he said. "We were never together. I've never been with Stephanie in that way."

"But there have been rumours about you and your brother's wife."

"And that's all they are...rumours. It sounds like you want to know about Stephanie so perhaps we ought to get her out of the way. On the night Brad died Stephanie had gone to my room whilst I was downstairs working. Brad found her in my bed but he was too incensed to reason or think logically. I heard them arguing and he must have stormed out of the house in a rage. What hurts the most was that he'd thought the worst and he never came to find me to ask if it was true. Brad came here, to the beach house, took the boat out and he never came back. I followed him down to the beach to explain but I was too late. He had vanished and I don't know if he meant to..."

Amy placed her fingers over his lips to silence him. There was no need for Max to say what he thought Brad had done. Max must have been devastated losing his twin brother in that way. And then she heard Max let out a deep sigh.

"Now I know how he must have felt when he thought someone he loved had betrayed him."

She realised Max was talking about James.

"James and I..."

"I was a fool. I now know about James and Cathy and I know you can never forgive me. And I don't expect you to forgive me for the things I said."

"You didn't know about James and Cathy?"

"No, I didn't. But that's no excuse for what's been said and done."

"Please Max...can we *not* talk about this?" she pleaded.

"I know it hurts you deeply and I know I've hurt you badly but we have to bring it out into the open or we'll never put it behind us. You might not want to talk about it now but there are things I need to tell you."

"Alright, I'm listening," she said. She clenched her hands into tight fists. She was waiting to hear the worst and scared of what she was about to be told.

Max took a deep breath.

"The shares..."

She stiffened, rigid with fear. She was remembering that dreadful night and she was fearful of what was to come.

"Max forget it. It doesn't matter," she said anxiously.

"Shut up and listen to me women. I need to tell you."

He ran a hand in frustration through his dark hair and then reached for her clenched fist.

Smoothing out her balled fist, he interlocked his fingers with hers and held onto her tightly.

He wasn't letting go.

Was he afraid she was going to run from him?

"The shares my mother made over to me...I've signed them over to Jake. I don't want them and I don't want you to think the shares are more important to me than you."

She was shocked and stunned by what he'd just revealed.

The man who had waited so long to gain overall control of the Jordan Diamond Empire had just told her he'd given the controlling shares away to their son.

"But why?" she asked. "You'll be in the same position as before. Stephanie can still threaten you and she could still take over the company."

"No, she won't be able to take over the company because I have a secret weapon to fight her with. I have you and I have our marriage," he said holding her close.

Max turned to her and looked deep into her soul.

"Amy, my darling, Amy. I can't take back what was said in anger that night and I can't take away your pain. I don't know if you can forgive me or if you'll ever give me your trust again...but I need you."

She didn't need to look at him to hear the sorrow and sadness in his words. And she didn't need to see him to witness his agony and torment.

She knew Max deeply regretted what had happen and she had to forgive him and let go of her hurt, otherwise, their relationship would be over.

They had to move on and move past what had happened.

Slowly she lifted her head and looked at him.

With nervousness and apprehension, she reached into her pocket and held out something precious towards him. It was something she'd been carrying with her since that night.

It was a small delicately wrapped package and Max reverently took it from her and carefully started to unwrap it.

"You never opened your second present that night, if you had, you would have known how I felt."

In his hand was the personalised gold keyring with its key-shaped disc that he had left unopened. When he saw the pictures of Amy and Jake inside and read the inscription - *you hold the key to our hearts* - his eyes filled with love.

Max kissed her gently and tenderly on the lips.

"Let's go home," was all he said.

EPILOGUE

Max and Amy were spending a night at home. Jake had been tucked into bed and was sleeping soundly and Alexander and Kim, having spent the weekend at the main house, had returned to the beach house.

Waterfront was back to normal.

Standing in the doorway of the master suite and silhouetted in the light from the passage, Max felt as if a weight had been lifted from his shoulders.

Before him, Amy was sitting at the dressing table carefully removing her makeup and preparing for bed.

As he looked at the woman he loved, he tried to remember what his life had been like without her. A few short months ago before their marriage, he'd been on his own with no one to share his thoughts with and no one at his side. Amy had changed all that. She had brought Jake into his life and he couldn't imagine life without them. She had become his soul mate and confidant.

"You do realise that you and Jake mean everything to me, don't you?"

There was desperation in his voice. For some reason, he needed to let her know how vital she was to his being. Without her he was nothing. He had nothing. There was nothing.

He entered the room and, firmly closing the door behind him, he walked towards the dressing table. Reaching for her, he tenderly and possessively pulled her back towards him. His arms went around her, circling from behind.

"You're mine and I want you all to myself. Is that so wrong of me?" he asked.

He planted soft, silky butterfly kisses along her jawline and nipped with his lips at the base of her long, slender neck.

"Max..." she whispered.

"Yes, my beautiful wife?" His voice was rough with emotion and desire.

His fingers began searching, caressing in intimate places. He was trying to distract her and he knew she was having difficulty thinking.

Reaching for the zipper on her dress and sliding it little by little down her back, he slowly exposed her soft, delicate skin to his caressing touch.

Unable to bear the torment any longer, Amy stood and turned towards him. As she turned, her dress fell away to the floor revealing the full roundness of her swollen breasts and her tall, slender body. He could never get enough of looking at her.

Gently she reached up and touched his cheeks and then he saw the seriousness in her eyes.

"Max, I will always be yours. Nothing can change that. Nothing can change my feelings for you. No one has my love as much as you."

"And I love you," he told her. "When I thought I'd lost you it was as if my world had ended. I love you so much. You'll never know how much."

But she did know.

He had proved how much he loved her four months ago when he'd willingly relinquished and signed over the extra shares his mother had given him to Jake.

It didn't matter that this week he'd been able to buy more Jordan Diamond shares when they had unexpectedly come onto the open market.

Stephanie had been selling her shares because she needed capital to invest in a project with her brother. Max had bought them, and with the new acquisition, he'd gained overall control and the security of the company was no longer at risk.

But that no longer mattered.

Max had already proved to himself, and to Amy, that the shares were not essential. To him, the shares had no true worth. What was of value was their love for one another, and for Jake. There was nothing more important.

"I do know how much you love me," Amy moaned as his mouth found hers.

His lips were forcing hers open and his tongue explored and teased before he licked his way to her breasts.

He was plundering and taking what she was offering.

"Oh, Max..." she cried out again as a shudder of excitement coursed through her. "Don't stop."

The moment he'd started to caress her, all coherent thought had vanished. The only thing that was of pressing urgency was to bury himself deep inside her womanly cavern.

His hands were running slowly over her body and he was arousing her. He was igniting her fire and bringing her to a familiar fever pitch of desire. Then he lifted her into his arms and carried her over to their bed and laid her upon it. She was trembling and her whole body was screaming with need.

Standing beside the bed Max hastily discarded his clothing until he was stood before her naked. He was ready but he needed a moment to simply look and revel in her beauty. He could see the longing in her eyes but he held back.

He was always amazed at how she could affect his potency. He only had to see her to want her.

Her physical beauty and the way she moved could instantly arouse him. And then, unable to wait any longer, they journeyed together and were taken to the heights and rapture of an all-consuming climax and release.

Spent and sated, and lying in each other's arms in the afterglow of their lovemaking, he pulled her close, cradling her into the warmth and comfort of his body.

"Were you really going to leave me?" he asked.

He was still tormented and often agonised about her disappearance on the night of his birthday.

"You told me to go."

"And you were going to leave me...and leave Jake behind?"

"I thought you didn't want me any longer," she confessed. "But that day on the beach, when you came to meet me, I had been thinking. I had decided I wasn't going to leave you after all. I couldn't leave you. I was going to take a risk and try and win back your love."

"You didn't have to win my love," he told her. "You've always had it. I've always loved you...and even when I thought you preferred James I still couldn't stop loving you."

"Shush..." she said and nestled closer.

"And how were you going to win my love back?" he asked.

He ran his fingers through her silky hair, caressing her softly.

"Like this...and like this..." she said. And as Amy planted a trail of fiery kisses along his jaw line, with equal passion, he returned her kisses; showing her his love deep into the night, over and over again.

About Arabella Sheen

Arabella Sheen is a contemporary and regency romance author of sensual, passionate love stories. She is a member of the Romantic Novelists' Association and was shortlisted for the RNA – Joan Hessayon Award.

Having worked for nearly twenty years as a theatre nurse in the amazing city of Amsterdam in the Netherlands, she now lives in the southwest of England with her family.

One of the many things Arabella loves to do is to read. And when she's not reading or writing romance novels, she is either on her allotment sowing and planting with the seasons or she's sitting on the sofa pandering to the demands of her attention-seeking feline.

You can find Arabella at the following places:
Website: arabellasheen.co.uk
Facebook: @ArabellaSheenAuthor
Twitter: @ArabellaSheen

Other Books by Arabella Sheen

Contemporary Romance - Sensual
Castell's Passion
Temporary Bride
Blinded by Desire

Regency Romance - Sweet
Westbury

Regency Romance Sensual
Westbury

**Please remember to review and rate your read.
All feedback is good feedback.
Thank you...**